BRAGAN UNIVERSITY SERIES
BOOK TWO

FIGHTING FOR YOU

GIANNA GABRIELA

COPYRIGHT

Fighting For You

Bragan University Series (Book Two)

Second edition, 2019

ISBN Ebook: 978-1951325053

ISBN Print: 978-1790318834

Cover design by Sly Fox Cover Designs

Edited by Lauren Dawes

DEDICATION

To My Mother.

Thank you for fighting cancer, Mom. I don't know what I would've done without you. You are the embodiment of a strong woman. You fought for not just yourself, but for me too.
I love you.

To Nayelis.

I know you're looking down on your family from heaven.

PROLOGUE

JESSE FALCON

Every time I near her door, I struggle to go inside. I hate being in the hospital. The smell is a mixture of things, all inescapable. The most prevalent is the jumble of two emotions—happiness and sorrow. Some people laugh. Some people cry; it all depends on the day.

I force myself to stand outside her door for a few more minutes. Who would've thought that I'd be here? Who would've thought I'd be spending my afternoons in a hospital entertaining her while she fights for her life? Not me. And I'm sure as hell she didn't expect to be here either.

No one should expect to be here because no one ever should.

Although my feet want to remain frozen, I take a deep breath and force myself to knock. I wait a few minutes, but no one answers. I press my ear to the door, hearing no noises coming from the other side. Maybe she's sleeping. *I should come back another time*, I tell myself but I know I'm just trying to find a reason not to go into that room.

Instead, I do what anyone in my position would do; I fight my cowardice, my desire to run away.

I open the door and let myself in. I'm immediately greeted by an empty space. Even for a hospital, it looks too clinical. The bed is made, the machines have been put away, and the flowers that were here yesterday are gone. There's no sign that someone was here. No sign that she had been here before.

Immediately, I get the feeling that something is wrong.

ZOE EVANS

Cancer.

That is the word ringing in my ears.

I have cancer.

Cancer.

Me.

I have it.

The word continues to loop like a bad sound track in my mind. It's on repeat, but I struggle to comprehend it. I hear my mother's cry, and turn in her direction just in time to see my father bringing his arms around her to keep her suddenly limp body from hitting the ground. *Her* reaction is what tells me I've heard the doctor right.

I think back at how I ended up here. One second, I was on the phone with my mother, telling her about this fever that wouldn't go away. Even with the fever, I remember telling her how excited I was to finally get a break from school and spend my time with her and dad. She kept insisting I get myself to the hospital, but I refused. I thought it was nothing... But it persisted. The fever didn't go away, so I finally decided to listen to my mother.

A fever. That's all I thought I had, but I was wrong.

I have Acute Lymphoblastic Leukemia.

Leukemia.

Cancer.

Me.

I have it.

The rest of the doctor's words are lost on me as I feel as if I'm not really in my body anymore, I'm not *in this room* anymore. Suddenly, I'm lightheaded and my vision blurs.

"Are you okay, Zoe?" I think I hear someone say, but before I can answer, everything goes dark.

1

ZOE

Three months. That's how long it's been since the day I arrived at this hospital. That's how long it's been since I was told that if I wanted to live, I was going to have to fight. I didn't get the luxury of just having a life; I had to work for it—I had to beat cancer.

I've had ninety days of treatment, each of which I've lived in a hospital, only seeing the outside world through windows and glass doors. With that passage of time, I've lost a lot, including the desire to continue fighting.

Doctors come in and out of the room like it's got a revolving door. That part hasn't changed since the day I arrived. Something else that hasn't changed is my parents. Well, I guess they've changed a little. They've become more informed, learned everything they could about Acute Lymphoblastic Leukemia. Not only have they made it their mission to educate themselves, but they've educated me on it too. They've even started calling it "ALL" which, they tell me, is the medical acronym for it. The doctors say ALL is the most common childhood cancer, and although I'm not a child, it didn't want to exclude me.

The crazy thing is that because ALL is a childhood cancer, the only place that can treat it is the Children's Hospital. So, despite being an adult, that's where I've been. In a way, I'm lucky that I'm in a place where the walls are brightly painted and the nurses are kind. Still, seeing other kids fight this disease is probably harder than seeing the adults. Kids have so much life ahead of them that they may not even get to live.

Another thing my parents told me is that cancer research funds don't necessarily award children's cancer research the same amount of money. When I found out why, I was pissed. Apparently, cancer research for children isn't a lucrative business since the kids can't pay for it. And when you're not old enough to vote, Congress doesn't give a shit about what happens. They don't answer to you, so they don't have to pass policies or budgets that will help find a cure. Instead, they hide under the excuse that "childhood cancer is rare" and so researching it doesn't make sense.

I think that's bullshit.

You know what else is bullshit? Watching my body deteriorate with each passing day. Seeing my hair fall out in chunks. I decided to just shave it off; it was easier that way. Instead of seeing red locks on my pillow or the shower floor every day, I saw just them all disappear at once. I ripped off the Band-Aid because they say it makes it easier... I'm not sure that it does.

I've seen every part of me that I love stripped away by this malicious illness. Still, my parents want me to follow the treatment plan, so I do. They want me to fight, so I do. I do it for them because if it was for me, I'd have given up a long time ago.

I've already finished the induction phase. In that phase, I was given intrathecal chemotherapy, which just means that the chemo was injected into my spine. As an added bonus, the drugs also cause my hemoglobin platelets and white blood cell counts to drop significantly. Now I need frequent blood and platelet transfusions in order to restore them. Hooray for needles.

I hate science—always have. But now, now I find myself interested in every aspect of it. Who would've thought cancer would do that? Anyway, the low counts and crappy immune system are the reasons why I haven't gone home yet.

I'm confined to this hospital—to this room.

My current round of treatment only makes it worse. I have to be isolated after every cycle of chemo so I can recover. Confined. Nauseated. Achingly lonely. After a while, the smells, the whiteness of my hospital room walls, the lighting in the room become almost unnoticeable. I wake up in the hospital every day, and while that made me anxious in the beginning, I've forgotten what it's like to not be here. Oddly enough, I even find myself missing the constant shuffling of the medical staff as they come in and out of my room.

This is my new normal.

Whenever the ban is lifted and I can finally have visitors—to see my family—I breathe a sigh of relief. I value every moment I get with my parents because I don't know which one may be the last. I miss them when they can't be near me.

I miss my friends, too.

They used to come and see me every day, but they've slowly stopped. At first, they would wait outside the door and the moment the doctors said it was okay for them to come in, they'd run into the room and take a seat next to my bed. But those visits became less frequent and, eventually, nonexistent. I don't blame them though. It's my fault. I've changed. Enduring this battle has changed me and not necessarily for the better.

For a long period of time, I stopped being the Zoe they knew— I'm still not. I was not the jolly, happy, enthused Zoe they had come to love. Instead, they saw a girl who had become a fraction of herself, one who'd lost all hope. After I found out I had cancer, Fear extend its hand to me and I took hold of it. I allowed it to lead me to the dark. I let myself become consumed by the illness and the very high possibility that I wouldn't overcome it. After that, I pushed my friends away little by little. Their jokes no longer made me smile. Their stories no longer interested me. And so eventually they stopped trying. They stopped showing up.

Now it's just me and my parents. Despite my constant mood swings, my parents are always there for me. They understand that I don't want to get my hopes up because if it doesn't work out, it'll wreck me. Literally. It doesn't mean they aren't hopeful. As I near the final leg of my treatment, they're praying it works. I'm praying too.

The doctors tell me I'll be able to go home soon. The treatment isn't over, but the last leg is a little easier. I'll have to return to the hospital every single day, and some days I'll even have to remain for a while longer, but it's something—small victories and all.

I'll take anything at this point. I'm even excited about getting to see a wall that isn't one of the ones I've been facing for the last few months. I can't wait to wake up in my own bed. I want to try and gather the pieces of my life, the pieces I'd abandoned when I didn't know if I would ever have the chance to live again.

I'm hoping I can put those pieces back together, but I'm also hoping that cancer doesn't tear apart the puzzle. Again.

2

JESSE

I turn off the shower, grab a towel and exit the shower rooms. Practice is over and while my body is screaming in pain, my mind knows I've gotta keep going. I can't stop now.

Work hard, play hard. That's supposed to be the motto of my life, except it couldn't be further from the truth. The summer has just started, but as both a football player and a pre-med student, this doesn't actually mean I'm free to do whatever I want.

In reality, it means the opposite.

Not only am I busting my ass running up and down the field for practices and scrimmages, but now I also get to run up and down the halls of a hospital for my internship. All for the sake of my future—an internship at the Children's Hospital that's wanted by many, but only given to a lucky few. I'd like to think the only reason I got it was because I earned it—because I work my ass off, that my grades are among the top of my class, but I'd be a fool to think my parents didn't influence the decision in some way. They're connected to this hospital and, in more ways than I'd like to admit, so am I. If it weren't for all of these things coming together, I wouldn't have the internship. I'm not sure I'd even want it.

"Are you good?" Colton asks behind me as I start changing into my scrubs.

"Yup, just running over to the hospital for the first day of my internship," I remind him.

"Think you'll be able to deal with being there every day?" he asks, and I know exactly why—he's worried.

"If I want to help fight cancer, I'm going to have to be," I assure him. Colton nods his head, seemingly content with the response I've given him—it's the same one I've used every time he's asked before. He knows me well enough to tell that I'm nervous and scared to return, but determined enough to push myself through it. I've been playing alongside him for a while now and I know he cares about each of us. Despite his sometimes... unfriendly demeanor, he's a brother to all of us—to me especially.

"Do you think you'll be good for practice tomorrow? I can tell Coach you've gotta miss it if you want?"

"I should be good. I signed up for this, so it's on me." I pat him on the shoulder. "Thanks though."

"No need. You know you're family."

"I appreciate that, man. How's Mia?' I ask, switching the subject. I retrieve my book bag from my locker and when I turn, I can see his expression has transformed—softened. The moment her name is mentioned, he turns into a different man.

I remember that feeling.

"She's good," he says, unable to stop himself from smiling.

"Good," I answer. I'm happy to see he's found happiness. I just hope he can hold onto it for as long as possible.

"Alright, well, I'll see you tonight," I add, turning towards the exit. I'm ready to get this first day over with.

"Maybe," he says and I shake my head without looking back at him. This means he'll likely be spending the night at Mia's. Since they've started dating, and in the aftermath of Abbigail, Colton and

Mia have been inseparable. The guys joke that we barely get to see him anymore. We all give him shit for it, but I think each of us have appreciated how Mia has made him a happier person.

I hop in my car, turn on the engine, and peel out of the parking lot. I drive to the hospital in silence, mentally preparing myself to take this on. I devise a game plan, trying to account for all possible contingencies. I tell myself that it's all going to work out. But, the closer I get to the hospital, the faster my heart beats. My pulse is racing and the fear is creeping in. I've driven this way too many times before, and while the reason I drive in this direction today is a little different, it isn't really. It's the same.

I park my car in the very familiar lot and open the door. After one final calming breath, I head towards the entrance. Despite the weight trying to hold my feet in place, I force one foot in front of the other and move towards the revolving doors. I know why I'm here. I know I have to be here if I ever want to become a doctor—I will become a doctor. I assure myself of these things with every step, convincing myself that turning around and walking away won't help me achieve my goal. It won't help me live up to my promise.

When I'm finally inside, I take a look at the interior, noticing all of the changes that have occurred since I was last here. The white walls are now covered with art. I guess it's to make it look livelier—less like a hospital. Another wall is painted with an ocean scene filled with a multitude of fish, coral, and sea life of all sorts. The other wall has a huge tree with bright red apples everywhere. I commend their efforts to make this place look less stoic. Children's hospitals aren't supposed to scare the children or be devoid of all creativity, art, and expression.

I take a deep breath and head straight toward the receptionist sitting at the front desk.

"Hi." I greet her with a shaky smile.

"Hello, how can I help you?" she answers with a smile of her own.

"My name is Jesse Falcon and I'm one of the interns starting today," I inform her.

"Oh yes!" she says, nodding. "You're the first to arrive. I'll let Dr. Roman know."

"Perfect, thanks."

She points at some chairs lining one side of the wall in the waiting room. "You can wait over there for her."

"Thanks," I say again, walking in the direction of the chairs. I sit in the closest one I can find. It's pathetic that as a six-foot-one, two-hundred-and-fifteen-pound football player I need to take a seat before my legs give out. But I can't help it.

"Calm down, Falcon. Stop being a coward," I mutter under my breath.

"Mr. Falcon?" a woman in a white coat says standing in front of me.

I jerk my head up. "Yes." I rise from my seat.

"I'm Doctor Roman," she says, extending her hand to me.

"Jesse," I tell her, shaking her hand. I smile awkwardly when

she gives me a knowing look after I introduce myself. Clearly, she already knows my name.

"Thank you so much for being here today. We're excited to have you as one of our interns this summer."

"Thank you for having me, ma'am."

"I see you've followed our instructions and have your scrubs on," she tells me with a warm smile.

"Just trying to fall in line." That's all I ever try to do.

"I can already tell everyone will love interacting with you— especially our patients, Jesse."

"I'm looking forward to it," I tell her though I'm unsure.

"I'd like to give you a quick tour of the hospital. The other interns won't be here for another week."

"Great," I tell her, following her lead.

"We'll start with the staff and then I want to give you a tour of the oncology unit. Based on your interest form, I think that's where you'll be spending most of your time."

"Sounds great." I say the words, trying to sound as excited as possible but knowing I'm not. It's a necessary evil. Something I have to do.

I follow behind Dr. Roman, trying to pay attention as she talks about the hospital's architecture, its history, the staff members, and some of the patients. She briefly mentions she knows my parents, which reminds me of how I managed to be here this summer. Despite my hesitance in coming, I hope to show her that I deserve my spot, that I didn't buy it. I'm here because of who I am, because of what I've been through, and that goes beyond my parents' network.

I tune out of the rest of the conversation as I'm too distracted looking around and taking in my surroundings, cataloguing the new additions to this place, while also remembering everything that remains the same. We walk by a hall, and I can see people standing outside of the doors. Some have their eyes closed, while others wipe away tears. The common thread is that they're all visibly tired, all fighting unimaginable battles. I look at them and then look away when memories start running through my head.

"Are you excited to begin?" Dr. Roman asks, clueing me back into the conversation.

"Extremely!" Again, I fake enthusiasm. I hope I'm a better actor than I think.

"Great. You have some paperwork to fill out and after that, you're free to go home. We'll start you tomorrow, and you'll just be assigned to this floor," Dr. Roman says, guiding me to the HR office.

"Thank you, ma'am."

"You're going to have to stop calling me *ma'am* at some point, son. 'Doctor' works. 'Roman' works. 'Stacey' works. Just not *ma'am*," she says with a carefree smile.

"Sorry, ma'am— I mean, Dr. Roman."

"That's better. This is your stop. I'll see you tomorrow," she says as we enter the Human Resources office.

"I'll be ready tomorrow," I tell her. Maybe saying it out loud will help me convince myself. That I can, in fact, do this.

"See you tomorrow, bright and early."

"See you then."

Hopefully.

3

ZOE

As I've done every day since I got the chance to go home, I arrive at the hospital and greet Rose, the receptionist. She gives me the sweetest of smiles and tells me she's happy to see me doing so well. She says that every day, and I think it's out of habit, or to make me feel better. I allow myself a moment to think about the fact that I *am* doing better than I was before. I also know the moment I enter the Poison Room, the feeling of doing well will change. I call it this because the drugs that are pumped through my veins not only kill the cancer cells, but also what little will I have left to keep fighting.

"Hey, Rob," I say, greeting the elderly man sitting just outside the Poison Room.

"Hey, Zoe. Nice to see you!" he answers animatedly.

"Good to see you, too," I reply. I see Rob all the time because he's always here. He isn't a patient, but his granddaughter, Maria, is.

"How's the treatment going?" he asks.

"Same old, same old. Just glad I get a break from the hospital stench," I respond, cringing at my own words. Here he is, stuck at the hospital because of his granddaughter and the only thing I can tell him is that I'm happy I'm not here.

"You can say that again," Rob says, surprising me with an understanding smile.

"How's Maria?" I ask.

"Grandbaby isn't doing too well, but God willing, she'll pull through," he says holding back tears I can see are ready to fall— tears I know he's shed before.

"She will," I assure him. I say it to comfort him because in reality I have no idea. I can only hope that she'll get to be a kid— to grow into a teen. Maybe she can. Up until recently, I didn't think I'd pull through. Sometimes I still think I won't—I may not. Maria, well she's been here for a few months more than I have. She was the first person I saw when I got here. One day, I heard her crying in the room next to mine and since that day I avoided it like the plague. When I heard her laughter resonate through the walls a few days later, I was drawn in.

Like me, Maria got the chance to go home a few months ago, but then she was brought back. The doctors said the treatment hadn't worked; she was relapsing. Now, she needs a bone marrow transplant and additional rounds of chemo. If those work, she'll get to live.

Rob comes to the hospital every day to give his daughter, Martha, a few minutes to step out of the room and breathe, and to spend time with his granddaughter. Despite his age, he's decided to donate bone marrow to Maria since he's a match.

I remember talking to Martha about the whole process a few weeks ago. She'd told me about what Maria was like before coming to this hospital. I loved hearing stories about her birthday parties. Martha also told me about losing her husband while he was deployed. Even while recounting this story to me, she remained strong. I could tell she was tired, and desperate for something to go her way, but that she wasn't going to complain. She was going to take it one day at a time and fight alongside her daughter. She's strong like that and I envied her optimism—her outlook.

"What are you doing out here?" I ask after a few seconds of silence. He rarely stays out in the waiting room; he's usually inside making Maria laugh.

"I just needed a quick break, but her mama is in there with her. She just went through another round of chemo... it breaks my heart to see her suffer," he says, tears finally gliding down his face. "I'm sorry," I tell him. I really am sorry that this is something she has to face, something anyone has to face.

"Me too. I would switch places with her in a heartbeat. She's got so much life left to live, and mine is coming to an end."

I pat him on the shoulder trying to comfort him. "I know you would. But don't say that, old man; you'll get a long life to enjoy watching Maria grow into a woman."

I take a seat next to him offering my silent support.

He smiles in between tears. "Thank you." My hand finds his and I hold onto the man who's become like a grandfather to me while I've been at this hospital. I remain quiet as there's nothing else I can say that'll make him feel better, nothing that'll stop Maria's suffering.

I silently pray for her treatment to work, for this family to once again find the joy that cancer has taken from them.

Fiona, one of the younger nurses, comes into the room and beckons for me to follow her. "Zoe, we're ready for you."

"Keep praying," I tell Rob as I take measured steps in the direction of the Poison Room. That's what my parents did—that's what my parents *do*. They pray it'll work.

JESSE

I STILL CAN'T BELIEVE I MANAGED TO GET MY FEET AND HEAD TO SYNC and take me to the hospital. My heart, on the other hand, wanted to stay as far from it as possible.

Today has been a little bit of everything. I've been running around the different floors trying to reorient myself with the hospital. In true intern fashion, I also made some coffee runs for a few of the nurses, and even some of the doctors. I didn't mind being an errand-boy because it was a built-in break—a chance for me to catch my breath.

After filling in wherever was necessary and doing some paper-work, Dr. Roman told me I was good to head over to the oncology floor and remain there for the duration of my internship. I won't be shuffling between floors and helping whoever needs me. Instead, I'm the sole property of the oncology unit. I know Dr. Roman is placing me there because she knows that cancer is my area of interest, and while I appreciate her for looking out for me, I'm overwhelmed at the idea of spending months on this floor–months watching patients go through different stages of treatment. I'm grateful for the opportunity, but at the same time just walking these halls brings back painful memories, but I know they'll compel me to do something.

"Have a seat," I hear one of the nurses, Fiona, I think her name is, say from right behind me as I finish cleaning up some of the equip-ment in the treatment room. "It's Jesse, right?"

I turn around, my eyes connecting with hers, but immediately jumping to the pretty redheaded girl standing next to her, her light hazel eyes a stark contrast to the fiery red of her hair.

"Hello?" Fiona adds impatiently.

"Yes, hi." I stumble on my words when I realize I haven't answered the nurse because I'd been staring at the girl for too long.

"Have you met Zoe yet?' she asks as the girl, Zoe, walks over to one of the chairs set up for chemo patients. She does it mechanically, like she's not in control of her own movements.

"No, I haven't. It's nice to meet you, Zoe," I say waving at her even though she doesn't seem to be aware of what's happening.

"Huh?" Her hazel eyes capture my own once again.

"Nice meeting you," I repeat.

"Is it?" she replies and I can't help cracking a smile.

Fiona says, "As you can probably tell, Zoe loves to be sassy."

"You love me and my sass," Zoe shoots back with a wink.

"You're not wrong," Fiona tells her and then adds, "Zoe has a few rounds of chemo left before she's done with her treatment. She's an outpatient who comes in for regular checkups each day. We schedule her for chemo rounds every couple of weeks, at which point she stays for an additional few days until we send her back home again."

I nod, following what she's saying like this is the first time I'm hearing it. The thing is, I know all too well what the process is like.

"Zoe's shown great progress and we're hopeful that the next few rounds of chemo will help," Dr. Roman says as she enters the room. She turns to the girl who clearly holds a place in both their hearts. "How are you feeling Zoe?"

"It's always a good day when I have to come to the Poison Room," Zoe responds and I chuckle. Everyone turns to me and I start coughing in a weak attempt to hide my outburst.

"Don't worry. After a while you get used to Zoe's sarcasm," Dr. Roman says.

"I'm sure going to miss it when you resume your life," Fiona says, bringing her hands to her hips.

"I'll come visit, don't worry. You guys won't get rid of me that easily," Zoe says with a sweet voice that has me paying attention to every word she utters.

"Have you met our intern Jesse?" Dr. Roman asks at the same time Fiona's pager beeps and she lets herself out of the room.

"I have, though I didn't know you had any interns," Zoe tells Dr. Roman. The two of them volley back and forth while I just stand there looking awkward as hell.

"We have a couple of spaces available over the summer for very special students. Jesse is actually a junior at Bragan University. You'll probably meet the girls later, but Jesse is who you'll see most often as he's assigned to this unit," Dr. Roman says while going through the chart in her hand.

They continue to talk as if I'm not in the room and I'm grateful for it because I've been too distracted by the way this girl smiles, the shade of red in her hair, the green in her eyes, and even the length of her eyelashes.

Stop being weird.

"Bragan University? That's awesome. I used to go there too!" she says, her voice laced with excitement, but there was also an undertone of sadness. She used to go to B.U. too. Probably before she had cancer. Probably before she was in this hospital. I'm instantly pissed at the thought that she too has had to miss out on things because of this illness—this disease.

"Really?" I ask.

"What? Do you think I'm not smart enough to be admitted?" she challenges.

"No, not at all—I—erm —I think you're great," I say before I can stop myself.

That was an odd freaking response.

"You think I'm great?" She repeats my words back to me, and I internally cringe.

"I—I can see you studying at B.U. I think you probably did well—will do well!" I add.

"Do well in what?" she questions, and boy if I'm not confused as to what the hell we're talking about.

"Let me start over." I take a deep breath. "It's great that you used to go there! Are you thinking about coming back after your treatment?" I ask.

"If the treatment works, then yes, it's a possibility."

"Um," I hesitate, unable to find the words I want to tell her. I want to assure her it will work and that she'll be able to come back to school, but I don't know if that's true. I can only hope it is.

"Sorry to interrupt, but Zoe we're ready to start you up on the chemo. Afterwards, we'll transfer you to one of the rooms and I think we'll keep you for at least two days to make sure everything looks good," Dr. Roman informs her, effectively putting an end to our conversation.

"Great! Can't wait!" Zoe says with fake enthusiasm.

"You're almost done," Dr. Roman assures her.

"Let's hope so," she says, a little more resigned. For a brief moment, I see the fear behind her eyes and it speaks to me.

"Jesse, could you please make sure Zoe knows what room she'll be in after chemo? I know her parents will be here afterwards and will want to know."

"Yes, ma'am," I respond, happy to leave the room. There's something about this girl that wakes some of the emotions I've had before. Her resignation to being ill makes this place feel a little more suffocating, and there's nothing I need more right now than air.

4

ZOE

I'm awoken by my aching body, and when I pry my eyes open, I realize I'm back in that room again—the room with the white walls and the beeping medical equipment. I turn to my right, finding my mother snuggled on the couch with a blanket thrown over her. Even in her sleep, worry lines frame her face.

The nausea hits me out of nowhere and I double over the bed, but nothing comes out. My stomach is empty. I wish it had something in it; I think it would feel better than dry-heaving.

"You doing okay, honey?" my mom asks sleepily as she lifts herself from the couch quickly. Her hand is on my back a moment later, her attempt to soothe me. "Want a ginger ale?" she adds when I don't respond.

"Yes, please," I tell her, tears sliding down my face. I can't stop them from falling despite how much I try—despite how strong I want to be.

"Coming right up," my mom answers, her eyes still bleary from an uncomfortable night on the couch. I'd try and get up and retrieve one myself, or even call a nurse over, but I know Mom wants to feel useful. I reposition myself on the bed after the nausea subsides.

"Hi," someone says from just outside the door.

I turn in the direction of the voice. "Hey," I say to the guy Fiona had introduced me to earlier. She'd told me the day before that someone new had started and she couldn't wait for me to meet him. Now I see why. He sure is easy on the eyes, and since Fiona is only a few years older than me, surely, she noticed too.

"Zoe, right?" he says, looking a little uncomfortable. I look him up and down. His blue scrubs hug his broad shoulders more tightly than normal.

"Yes. Could you remind me your name again?" I ask him. It feels like I was introduced to him days ago instead of just yesterday. Yesterday, I was so focused on what followed the chemotherapy that I didn't care about anything else.

"Already forgotten, huh? I guess I wasn't that memorable," he says, cracking a smile. I find myself smiling too, unable to resist his charm. "I'm Jesse." He extends his hand to me.

I look down at the blanket covering my legs. "This is embarrassing, but I may have been throwing up a few minutes ago so I don't think you'll want to shake my hand."

"Nonsense," he says, getting closer to the bed, his hand still extended.

"Are you sure?" I look at him, waiting for him to change his mind.

"You're not contagious, are you?' he says with a chuckle.

"Not that I know of, but who knows? Maybe that's how I got ALL in the first place," I joke, but I can see his eyes harden. It passes just as quickly as it comes, though, and he takes my hand in his own, shaking it.

"I'm don't think that's how it works," he tells me, still holding onto my hand. I feel the roughness of his fingers, and the massiveness of his palms.

"I'm sorry I didn't remember your name. I wasn't paying too much attention yesterday," I tell him sheepishly.

"I wouldn't have been able to tell," he retorts and I can see in a different world, like in a world where a guy like him would look at a girl like me, or where I wasn't sick, we'd be good friends.

"You're going to have to start paying attention if you're thinking about returning to B.U.," he tells me, then realizes he's still holding my hand. He lets go, a blush creeping up his neck and shading his cheeks.

"I think I'll manage. It was nice seeing you again, Jesse," I tell him.

I watch as he takes a few steps back and stands awkwardly near the door. I can tell he's debating whether he should stay or leave. He seems a little flustered, which is surprising considering how handsome he is. I wouldn't have pegged him as a guy who easily gets nervous. With his ocean blue eyes, dark brown hair, and even wearing his scrubs, I'd think he'd confidently command every room he walks into.

Instantly, I wish I'd met him under different circumstances. I wonder if we'd both attended B.U. at the same time, would we have run into each other in the quad, café, or at a football game? I'm sure he's an athlete. I mean, with that frame it'd be a waste not to be.

"How are you feeling?' he asks, lingering longer despite being given a chance to get out. I guess he does have a job to do; he isn't here for a social visit.

"I feel the same as usual," I tell him. He once again abandons his spot near the door and moves towards me.

"So there's the nausea, which you already told me about, but what else is there? Weakness in your limbs? Headache?" he asks, and I notice he's not looking down at the paper in his hand.

"*Ding! Ding! Ding!*" I joke, feeling myself get light-headed almost immediately.

"Sweetie, I've got your ginger ale. Sorry it took so—" my mother says, stopping when she sees Jesse. I look up to find her staring at him.

"Hello, dear. I'm Danielle," my mom says, extending her free hand to Jesse while handing me the ginger ale.

Avoiding her eyes like she's the most intimidating person he's ever met, he mumbles, "It's nice to meet you, ma'am. I'm Jesse— one of the interns."

I hold back a giggle at how visibly red this guy is getting and take a sip of my ginger ale. I really hope it'll push away the nausea and somehow miraculously give me strength. The room goes completely silent while my mom watches him with curiosity. He looks to me then back to her. I can physically feel his discomfort. Under different circumstances, this would've been hilarious, but right now it's just awkward.

"I was just checking in to make sure Ms. Evans was doing okay," he says, answering a question she never asked.

"And is she?" my mom asks with a big smile.

"I am," I tell her, relieving Jesse of any further questioning and giving him yet another opportunity to escape.

"On that note, I'll be back a little later to check in," he says, striding through the door.

"Cute guy," Mom says with a glint in her eye that tells me she's up to no good.

"No!"

She lifts her eyebrow questioningly. "Not cute?"

"Not happening. Whatever's going through that head of yours it is not happening, Mom!"

"There was nothing in my head," she says, but her smile tells me she's lying through her teeth.

"You've never been a good liar," I tell her.

"All I'm saying is he's a handsome guy," she says innocently.

"And?" I ask, though I know I shouldn't.

"And nothing. Don't you agree?"

"I guess, Mom. Yes, he's a little attractive."

She claps in excitement. "You should get his phone number!"

"And do what with it? You see; I knew you were up to something!"

She points at herself. "Who? Me?" she says, acting innocent. "I was just thinking it might be good to get yourself some new friends," she says, and while I know she's joking, I also know her words are true.

"He's just doing his job, Mom. I'm sure he doesn't need any new friends."

And even if he did, I don't want to be the burdensome sick girl to anyone else ever again.

Burdening my parents is enough. My friends couldn't take it and I won't make anyone else go through that.

"Doesn't hurt to try, Zo," my mom continues, pulling a chair closer to my bed.

"It ain't gonna happen, Mom!"

"Fine. But you're no fun—you get that from your father. If you were anything like I was when I was your age, his number would not be the only thing you'd be getting."

I gasp in mock horror. "Mom! Gross! We've talked about you telling me stories of your 'adventurous' youth!"

"I'm not giving you any details. I'm just saying, live a little," she says, wiggling her eyebrows.

If I get the chance to, I will. I'm prepared to live a little more, but only when I know I'm actually going to live.

The jury's still out on that one.

My mom takes a seat on the couch, grabs the remote and turns on the TV. She begins flipping through the channels, stopping only when she finds FRIENDS. This has become our ritual from the first day we walked into this hospital. She always sits next to me, while I lay in the hospital bed. With her hand clinging to my own like a lifeline, we watch FRIENDS until Dad shows up a little later. Somehow, this helps us think about the better times in our lives—the times before this.

FRIENDS begins and I can't help but remember when I had some of my own.

5

JESSE

I'm not sure if I'm actually allowed to check on patients yet. Still, after I found out which room Zoe was in last week, every time I walk by, it's like a magnet pulling me in her direction. All I know is I want to see her again.

For the majority of my morning, I shadow a few different doctors, making sure I don't give into the urge to check on Zoe; I remind myself that she isn't exactly my responsibility. Even if she was, it was so hard to find the courage to knock on her door the first time around that I don't know if I could do it again. Though seeing her smile might be worth it.

Still, I wasn't prepared for her mom to watch my every move— or even be in the room—while I stumbled through a conversation with her daughter. I couldn't help the nerves that took over. I felt like a school boy meeting my girlfriend's parents for the first time. But that wasn't actually the case.

Her mom showing up was not something I was expecting, but I

should have. Parents tend to spend every waking moment here. Who wouldn't want to make sure that their child is okay? Cancer affects them just as much as the patient—maybe even more because watching something happen to someone they love, knowing there's nothing you can do about it, fucking hurts.

The similarities between suffering parents is striking, but not shocking. Zoe's mom has bags under her eyes, and looks visibly tired. I know her exhaustion is both physical and emotional.

"There's one more patient you all haven't met yet!" Fiona tells me when I walk by the nurse's station. "Follow me," she adds cheerfully.

Since I started a little over a week ago, I've discovered she is, in fact, not only a nurse, but also the intern coordinator. Following behind her are Lilly and Marissa, the other two interns who joined us yesterday. I found out they're both already in the medical program at Bragan—which is a difficult thing to do considering the school accepts less than twenty percent of applicants. I asked them both a few questions about the program, and how they found the process of getting in since that's what I want to do after graduation.

It seems it won't be too hard to get some insight about the application process because, although they both seem to be quite bright—they have to be if they're in the medical program at B.U.—Lilly couldn't stop making eyes at me while Marissa flipped her hair flirtatiously after answering all of my questions. I'm not an idiot. I can tell when someone's feeling me and they both were. But, while I appreciate the compliment, I'm more interested in how they got into the med program than I am in getting their phone numbers.

Lilly and Marissa walk next to me as we follow Fiona, and every so often I hear them whisper then giggle about something. I walk faster, matching Fiona's speed and catching up to her.

"Okay, we're here!" Fiona says as we arrive in room 201. "Before we go in, let me tell you about who you'll be meeting. Her name is Maria and she's been a patient here for almost a year. She's four years old. She'd responded well to the treatment, but ultimately relapsed a couple of months ago. Right now, her grandfather is donating bone marrow to hopefully save her life." Fiona's eyes get visibly teary as she speaks. I feel my hand twitch at my side, knowing it's because I feel powerless to change her reality. I guess it doesn't get any easier with time.

"Poor baby," Lilly says to Marissa in an audible whisper.

"I can't imagine what she's going through," Marissa adds, equally distraught.

"You won't have to imagine it because you're going to see it every day," Fiona responds and while that may sound insensitive, I know she's right. "Anyway, Maria is a sweetheart and I wanted her to meet you all. She's one of those patients you'll want to come and say hello to every so often." We all nod.

"Treatment isn't the only thing these kids need; they also need someone to make them laugh, someone to make them smile and to forget they're sick, even if just for a few minutes." Fiona looks at each of us intently and then adds, "This part of the job is just as important as all others. We never know when the last smile will be, so we make each of them count." Fiona takes a moment to compose herself. One thought loops through my mind: Cancer doesn't tell you when it's going to take away the people you love. It just does it.

"Let's head inside," Fiona says finally. She knocks on the door before opening it and we all follow after her.

ZOE

Maria bursts out laughing as we play peek-a-boo. It's kind of crazy how easy it is to entertain kids. Even in this place, they don't lose the innocence they had when they first walked in. Maria's laughter echoes off the walls and we all laugh along with her.

I turn when I hear a faint knock and watch Fiona walk in with a smile on her face. Trailing behind her are two girls wearing scrubs. One is a brunette and the other one is blonde. Rob, Martha, and

Maria turn in the direction of the door as Fiona greets everyone. "Nice to see you making your rounds, Zoe," Fi tells me with a wink.

"She always does. You guys should hire her," Rob jokes.

"I'll let you know when I'm looking for a job," I answer.

"We'll be sure to save it for you," Fiona replies and we all laugh. I don't know that I'd ever want to work here. It may be selfish, but I don't want to see people suffering.

"Rob, Martha, Maria, these are our new interns—Lilly, Marissa, and Jesse," Fiona says just as Jesse steps into the room.

"Very nice meeting you all," the small blonde says a little too cheerfully. I don't know if she's Marissa or Lilly.

"Yes, happy to meet you," the other one adds, her voice high-pitched.

"How's the little one doing?' Jesse asks, looking directly at Maria, who has since fallen asleep. She looks peaceful like that and I watch her for a beat.

"She's doing okay. She was laughing right before you guys came in, but you know how fatigue comes out of nowhere. We're just getting ready for her transplant," Martha says, running her fingers through her daughter's brown hair lovingly. Maria is Martha's everything. I'd recognize that look anywhere because it's the same one my mother gives me—the look that shows they'd give anything to switch places with us.

"Good to hear," Jesse says, and I can tell he's going to be a good doctor. His eyes find mine, and for a moment all I can do is stare, trying to figure him out. I break the connection and turn my attention to Fiona instead.

"What brings you all here?' Rob says.

"Lilly and Marissa are med students at Bragan; Jesse is pre-med there too," Fiona explains. I know he's an intern at the hospital and all, but with his build, I'd peg him for someone who'd want to play a professional sport full-time instead of subjecting himself to an extremely hard program. I knew a few students in the program who complained about the harsh load of work they had and how difficult it was to get in.

I watch him subtly, tracing the muscles visible through his scrubs. Men in uniform have always done it for me—I never thought scrubs would have the same effect though.

"So, you all want to be doctors?" Martha asks, finally tearing her eyes off Maria and engaging in the conversation. "Do you have a specific field in mind?"

"I want to go into physical therapy," the blonde replies.

"I want to go into sports medicine," the brunette adds, and at her response I shake my head. I don't mean to be one of those girls who judges others without knowing them, but for some reason with these girls I can't help it.

"So why are you here?" I ask. "I mean, this is the oncology floor at a children's hospital." This isn't the place you go to for physical therapy or sports medicine. None of us are fancy sports players... Well, maybe Jesse is, but he isn't a patient.

"Um," is the only sound that comes out of the blonde girl's mouth as she's stumped by my question. She looks to the brunette for help, but her friend doesn't offer anything in response either. Their discomfort doesn't make me feel bad. Instead, it confirms what I already know: they don't want to be here, at least not long- term. For them, this is temporary. This is their way of meeting whatever academic requirement they have before moving on to the kind of work they want to do—the kind of medicine that pays them well and keeps them away from children sick with cancer.

Temporary for them. Permanent for us, I think bitterly.

"You didn't answer the first question," I say to Jesse when I realize the girls won't say anything else.

"Me?" he asks, pointing at himself.

"Yeah, you." I don't know why I'm so invested in this topic. I guess I want to know if this is temporary for him too.

"I'm hoping to go to med school and do cancer research," Jesse responds, not missing a beat. He scratches his hair as he waits for whatever's coming next.

"Wonderful," Martha says with a hopeful smile taking back control of the conversation.

"We need more people like you, young man," Rob tells Jesse, echoing my thoughts. "More good people who want to help those that are suffering."

"All I want to do is help in whatever way I can, sir," Jesse tells Rob and they both share a nod of understanding.

"Well, we're off to go and visit a few other patients today!" Fiona announces. "Please let us know if you need anything."

"Will do. Thanks for everything!" Martha tells an already retreating Fi.

"Stay out of trouble, Zoe," Fiona warns me, pulling open the door. The girls follow behind, and just as before, Jesse's the last to leave. I see his gaze turn to Maria once more. Then it bounces to Martha, Rob, and finally to me. He opens his mouth like he's about to say something else, but then shuts it, shakes his head and gives a little wave goodbye before following the others out.

6

JESSE

The all too familiar sound of gravel crushing beneath my feet fills my ears. The sun is hidden, the clouds taking over and painting the sky a lifeless gray. According to my weather app, there's also an impending rainstorm—this couldn't be more perfect.

I take cautious steps to where I know she is, following the pebbled path to where she...where the love of my life has been for a few years now.

Arriving at the stone marked with her name, I take a deep breath, and allow my fingers to trace the outline of her name, the tips following each letter. '*Hayley Evergreen. 1996-2014 Amazing daughter, sister, friend. Gone too soon.*' Those were the words chosen to be on her epitaph. I had no input when it came to choosing them. It's not that I wasn't asked—more like I was in denial that she was really gone. I had been for a while, but ultimately, I accepted it. If I'd chosen anything to add to her epitaph, I would've added *girlfriend* to the list of things.

I lower myself to my knees, removing the now wilted flowers I'd brought her last week. I replace them with a new bouquet of lilies—her favorite. I take a seat next to her headstone and start to talk. "I can't believe it's almost been four years, Hayley." I know she can't hear me, but maybe she's listening from somewhere up above.

"I started my internship this week. It was interesting being there again—and by interesting, I mean terrifying. If you'd been here, you'd have told me to suck it up, to get over my fear and move forward—to move on. Then again, if you were here, I wouldn't need to be there. I may have chosen a different path, another career."

"So, I met this little girl, Maria. You'd love her; she's adorable and has the prettiest smile. She's four years old and her laughter is contagious. Actually, she reminds me a little of you, of what I imagine you were like when you were her age. I always thought you were the kind of girl to wear your mother's dresses and dance around the house all day."

I clear my throat, stretching my legs out in front of me. Turning my head to the side, I trace the letters of her name with my eyes. "Remember when I asked you to prom?" Hayley had been dropping hints for weeks, waiting to see when and if I'd be asking her. The guys had given me so much shit for waiting so long.

The thing is, I wanted to take my time. I needed to do it right because you only got to ask a girl like Hayley once. And if you were going to dare ask, it had to be perfect. Not because she demanded it, but because she deserved it. She was the girl of my dreams—she still is.

I'd met her in middle school. She'd transferred in after her parents divorced. I couldn't describe how seeing her for the first time had made me feel—the eleven-year-old me didn't have the words. I just knew there was something special about her. Her smile made me smile. Her kindness made me want to be better. I remember sitting next to her in class and listening to her go back and forth with the teacher about climate change. The teacher didn't know what to do with her; she was so full of passion and wouldn't back down. I knew she was the kind of girl who made those around her better.

Even though I was young, I knew she was meant to be my girl. She cared about everything. She wanted to change the world; I saw her as my world.

So yeah, if I was going to ask her to prom, I was going to make damn sure I did it right.

"Setting up the *promposal* was terrifying. You were going to hang out with some of your friends—a girl's day out you called it. I took advantage of the fact you weren't going to be home. I talked your mom into letting me use your home for the best *promposal* ever. Although your mom was hesitant after I told her the plan, she eventually got on board. I said I wanted to make it the best night you ever had."

I chuckle as I recall the look on her face. "At first, she thought I was talking about sex and after I spent a few minutes—a few long awkward minutes explaining myself—I convinced her otherwise."

"I set up string lights all around your house. I placed candles from the entrance all the way to your back patio. Your mom wanted to help, but I insisted on doing it myself. She kept gushing about how sweet the gesture was and only after she reassured me everything looked amazing did my nerves settle a little. Then, she left me at your house while she went to meet a friend. She entrusted me with her little girl, and I knew I'd never do anything to ruin that."

"I still can't believe she just let me roam your home freely without supervision. I could've burned the place down!"

"When your friends were on their way to drop you off at home, they sent me a warning text as planned. As soon as I saw it, I lit all the candles, unlocked the front door, and got into position. The candles guided you to find me on my knees. I told your mom I should've proposed to you instead but, as expected, she shut that idea down really quickly. If I'd known your life was going to be as short as it was, I would have..." I pause and look up at the sky.

I push the thought out of my mind. "I don't blame your mom for saying no; you were seventeen years old. I couldn't give you everything you deserved. Not then. I just wish I could have. I wish I'd married you when I had the chance." I grab one of the small pebbles off the ground and toss it in the air, catching it without looking.

"You gasped the moment you opened the front door, and I assumed it was because of all of the candles. I recall hearing your rushed steps, your voice getting closer and closer. You called out for your mom, and I just waited patiently—nervously."

"The look on your face when you saw me on one knee, holding a corsage in one hand and a painted canvas in the other which read 'Dance the (Prom) Night away with me?' was priceless. I stood up and you walked into my arms, all still without giving me an answer. When you finally said yes, I spun you around, just listening to your rich laughter filling the air. It was music to my goddamn ears." I bring my fingers to my face and wipe away a stray tear. Even now, even after so long, they still make an appearance whenever I come to this place.

I look up to the sky again, hoping that Hayley is looking down on me and I utter the same words I tell her every time I come to visit her grave.

"I miss you." So damn much.

ZOE

If you asked me to define chemotherapy, I'd tell you it's the act of pumping poison into a human body with the hopes it'll kill the other poison before it kills the person.

It's much like picking your poison, except I don't feel like I had much of a choice.

I wish I had a choice, but the truth is that even if I did, I wouldn't know what to choose.

I sit here in the same room, facing the same wall, even sitting in the same chair like I do every time. The machines continue to beep as I wait for the drugs to make their way into my body. I'm even ready for the nausea, light headedness, dizziness, and everything else that comes with it.

I pray it works because if it doesn't, I don't know what else I'd be willing to do.

I shift around in the chair desperate to find some comfort, but nothing I do can make it better.

Just another day. Just another round.

It seems as if there's always just one more thing.

The doctors describe me as 'lucky' because I came to the hospital when I thought I just had a fever, which gave them the opportunity to diagnose the cancer before it was too late. Apparently, most people ignore the symptoms because they're so common. At least my cancer is still treatable...at least that's what the doctors tell me. They hope the chemotherapy makes a difference and I don't have to get a bone marrow transplant. My parents hope it doesn't get that far. I just hope it's not false hope.

"Hey, sweetie," my mother says coming into the Poison Room.

"Hi, Mom," I respond tearing my eyes from the IV and focusing on my loving mother instead.

"Where's your hat?" she asks, searching the immediate surroundings.

"I left it in the room."

"Aren't you cold?" I can hear the concern in her voice.

"I'm good." I smile at her. I can't help but remember the day chemo started. I can't erase from my mind the memory of waking up and finding clumps of hair on my pillow. Red hair lying on top of the sheets. Red everywhere. It took me a few minutes to realize it was my hair. I'd forgotten that chemo does that too—causes your hair to fall out. So, when I saw it was happening to me, I cried. That was my immediate reaction. Then, I did something about it.

I had my dad bring in his razor and shave my head. After it was done, I felt better.

"You're such a strong girl," my mother tells me, grabbing a nearby blanket and throwing it over me.

People keep saying I'm strong: the doctors, nurses, my father's coworkers, my mother's friends. Everyone. But I don't feel strong and, to be honest, I don't want to be.

Strength comes from choosing to stand up against something. Well, if I had a choice, I'd likely succumb to the illness instead.

I close my eyes and wait for the chemo dose to finish, knowing what waits for me on the other side isn't much better.

7

ZOE

After a long three days in the hospital, the doctors have cleared me to go home, assuring me that the chemo's effects are done—for now. I'm free to spend the rest of the time in my house—in my room. The definition of freedom is different to everyone, I guess.

My freedom will be short-lived though; I'm due to return to the hospital tomorrow, and the next day, and the next. Still, I get to sleep in my own bed.

"Ready to go?" Mom asks me, a huge smile pasted on her face. She's smiling because after a couple of rough days, I finally feel better again. And when I feel better, she does too.

"Where's dad?" I ask, looking in the direction of the door.

"He's downstairs in the car," she says bouncing on the balls of her feet. I can't count how many times I've told her to calm down, that this isn't the end, but there's no point. She loves celebrating the small wins.

"Okay," I tell her as she starts clearing the room of all of my personal belongings. At this rate, the hospital should just keep this room reserved for me since I'll be spending a couple of nights a week in this place anyway.

"What do you want to do on your first night back home?"

Mom asks, stuffing a blanket into one of my old gym bags. I roll my eyes because she asks me this question every time. I was home three days ago, but to her, every night I return is something worthy of celebration.

"There's not much I can do Mom, remember? Doctors' rules and all," I remind her. But then I see her smile fall a little, I immediately regret raining on her parade. I don't mean to be cruel, but we need to be aware of what's happening, of what could happen.

"Friends and pizza then?" she asks, smiling again and I smile back. Without her constant light, all of my days would be filled with darkness.

Someone clears their throat and I glance at the door to find Jesse standing there. I may be sick, but I'm not blind. That boy is hot.

"Can I come in?" he asks, shifting from foot to foot.

"Seems like you already did," I tell him, pointedly looking at his foot over the threshold.

"Oh, my bad—I'm sorry," he mutters, taking a step back and effectively removing himself from the room.

"You should be," I tease.

"Young lady! You need to be kind," my mom reprimands and I burst out laughing. She knows I'm joking, but the way Jesse looks right now makes me think he doesn't.

"That was me being kind, mom; you know that!" I smile and Jesse chuckles but doesn't close the distance. I stare at him expectantly, lifting my brows to indicate he should let himself in.

"You really need to get better at just entering rooms," I tell him.

"Would it be—"

I sit up slowly, dangling my legs off the side of the bed. "Get in already."

"Hi," Jesse says his eyes looking directly at me and I tilt my head to the right finding myself fixating on the dimple on his cheek.

"I'll go get the release papers from the front desk," my mom says, scurrying out of the room. She looks back from behind Jesse's large frame and winks at me. I know that the moment we get home—and away from dad who still looks at me like I'm five—she's going to be grilling me about him. I know she'll question his 'intentions', ignore my answers, and come up with her own conclusions.

"Hello."

I roll my eyes at him greeting me again "There's that word again," I tell him.

He takes a few steps closer. "Sorry. Dr. Roman wanted me to stop by and ask if you have any other questions before you head out."

"Nope. I know I'm basically not allowed to do anything. I have to wear a mask while I'm at home. I can't have any visitors… I'll be living in my own personal sterile bubble. Did I miss anything?"

"I think you've got it down pat," he says with a blinding smile.

"I've done it enough times." *Too many.*

"Only a few more weeks," he says, trying to make me feel better. I echo his words, not really believing them.

"You can have friends over. They just need to wear masks too."

"I don't have to worry about friends showing up. They sort of left weeks after I became the Girl with Cancer," I say and immediately cringe. Why am I sharing this much of my life with him? I didn't even tell my parents why my friends stopped showing up. But with this guy, I'm apparently in a soul-bearing mood.

"Are you serious?" he asks, his voice clipped, his eyes growing dark. I look down at his hands, clenched at his sides. I must have struck a nerve.

He probably pities me.

"Yes, really," I say, pretending it doesn't affect me. "I'm sorry I shared that. I don't usually tell strangers my life story." I glance up at him. "I don't want your pity either," I snarl. "I'm not broken."

"I… I don't. Pity doesn't do shit. I just can't fathom why your so-called friends would leave you when you need them the most. Those are the kinds of people I pity." Jesse stops and takes a deep breath before adding, "They weren't friends to begin with, you know?" His tone has changed to something I can only describe as sweet. I look down to find he's no longer balling his hands into fists.

I nod. "I know that now." I've learned that regardless of how tough things get, friends don't leave you behind. Friends pick each other up. They should have called me out on my attitude– not abandoned me.

"Also, feel free to share anything you want with me. I'm not a stranger, remember. I'm your Good Doctor," Jesse says, causing me to laugh out loud.

"Intern, you mean?" I correct.

"Good Intern, hopeful Good Doctor?" he says, smiling, and I'm afraid to admit I'm a little taken by him. A school girl crush— that's what I'd call it.

"Maybe one day," I tell him.

"Definitely one day."

"You're sure about that?" I don't know that I've ever been as certain about anything as he seems to be about becoming a doctor.

"I've only been sure about one other thing in my life," he says, his mood clearly darkening once again. I wonder what that other thing is, and find myself about to ask when my mother walks back into the room.

"Ready to go?" she asks, unaware of the moment she's just interrupted.

"Yep," I tell her, getting up from the bed.

Jesse takes my elbow, gently guiding me off the edge of the mattress. "Good luck at home. If you need anything, or feel like anything's wrong come straight to the ER. Don't risk anything. A fever, a long-lasting headache, nausea, whatever it is. Come to the emergency room. And, if you need anything else—don't be afraid to let me know," he says to me. He sounds like a parent making sure their child is aware that they can't stay out past curfew—no excuses.

"Yes, Doctor," I joke.

"Does she have your number, young man?" my mom asks, and I turn to glare at her. *What the hell is she doing?*

"She does not," Jesse responds shyly.

Mom's hands go straight to her hips as she successfully embarrasses me. "So how does she get in contact with you?"

"He was just saying that, Mom. He meant the hospital!"

"What? I mean, he said let him know." She looks at me like it's obvious that I need his personal phone number.

"That's true, ma'am. I'll write my number down and you can give me a call if you need anything. Remember, I'm not a doctor—"

"Not yet," I interrupt.

"I'm not a doctor *yet*, so if anything, head straight to the hospital."

"Yes, sir," I joke, glad we've moved past the awkward mom-getting-hot-guy's-number-for-me moment.

"I'm serious, Zoe. Please be careful," he says, handing me a piece of paper I didn't realize he'd ripped from his notepad.

"She will be," Mom answers on my behalf smiling widely as she looks at the paper in my hand.

"Do you have any other questions? I may not have the answer, but I can ask someone that knows," he says, looking at my mother first and then back at me.

"Are you an athlete?" she blurts out. The question has clearly been running through *my* mind, but I didn't think it was appropriate to ask. Of course, *my mothe*r has no fear whatsoever—and no filter either.

"Yes, ma'am. How'd you know?" He looks directly at me and I blush in response. From the corner of my eye, I catch my mother giving me a knowing look.

"Just wondering, sweetheart," she says innocently.

"What sport do you play?" If we're going to do this, we might as well go down the road fully.

"Football," he answers and I nod because that's exactly what I expected him to play.

"What position?" I continue the conversation like my father isn't waiting for mom and me in the parking lot—like Jesse doesn't have other patients to see and things to do.

"Kicker, actually." I can't stop my eyes from slowly shifting down to his legs. Football players have great bodies, but kickers have amazing legs. His scrubs don't give much away, and I find myself wishing I'd run into him at the beach.

"From what I know about football, which isn't much by the way, the kicker is really important. Field goals, punts, kickoffs and all," I tell him, but it comes out more like a question and his eyebrows rise in surprise.

"You know enough to know the right terminology. That's more than most girls..." He coughs, "Sorry—*people* I meet."

"Eh, you look like a football player by the way," I tell him and curse internally for letting those words escape my mouth.

He gives me a knowing smile. "I do? I hope that's a compliment."

"I don't know. It could be." I try to course correct, but it's too late. I've complimented the guy and there's no way I can take it back.

"I'm sorry to cut your flirting short, but your dad just sent me seven text messages in a row. He's getting impatient," my mother says.

"Mom!" I shout. "Not flirting!"

"Of course you weren't," she says sarcastically.

Jesse apologizes, and I'm not sure if it's because he thinks he's making us late, or if he considered what we were doing flirting.

"You have no reason to apologize," I tell him. I enjoyed our conversation. There's so much more about him I'd like to know, and I don't understand why I find myself invested in him. Maybe it's because he's the only other person that's around my age.

"You sure don't," Mom adds, looking up from her phone.

Argh, could this get any more awkward?

"We've got to go, Jesse. Mom is getting to the age where she can't tell the difference between people talking and flirting."

"Girl, I've done my fair share of both and can tell the difference from miles away!"

WTF, Mom?

I shake my head, silently begging for her to understand. "Please stop."

"I'm just saying. This," she says, pointing at both of us, "is great.

You'll just have to do it on a different day. Maybe you can text Jesse tonight and he can come over for dinner or something."

I hook my arm with hers and begin to pull her out of the room. "We're leaving now."

Turning back, I mouth, "I'm so sorry about her."

He chuckles, a laugh so rich that I feel it in the depths of my stomach.

"No worries," he mouths back. "See you tomorrow."

"See you then," I answer. Mom and I reach the elevator bank and I press the button for the lobby where dad awaits.

I'm shocked because for the first time in a while, I'm actually looking forward to tomorrow.

Even more surprising is that I'm looking forward to coming back here.

8

ZOE

"I haven't seen you in a couple of days, where have you been hiding?" Jesse asks coming into the room I'm staying in. I had chemo again this week and as usual, after I'm treated, I stay in the hospital for a couple of nights so they can keep an eye on me and the chemo's effects.

"I could say the same about you!" I respond.

"They've been keeping me busy. I had to help out on a different floor," he says, seemingly disappointed.

"That makes sense. Welcome back."

He shakes his head and smiles, "You didn't call me."

"I thought you said to call if I felt bad," I respond.

Shaking his head, he chastises, "I said go straight to the emergency room if you feel bad and to call me if you needed anything else."

"Right," I tell him, because that's *exactly* what he said.

"I'm glad you're okay. How are you feeling?" he asks.

I look around the room, mulling the question over before bringing my attention back to him. “I’m okay,” I answer.

Nodding, he absently plays with the hair on the back of his head before speaking again. “Good. You’re nearing the end.”

“That’s what you guys tell me.”

He stares at me intently for a moment. “Do you think it’ll be okay if I stopped by during lunch?” he asks shyly.

Grinning, I say, “Do you want to be friends with me or something?”

“Something like that. You’re like the only one my age around here.”

“Oh, so you’re saying if it weren’t because we’re around the same age, you wouldn’t bother talking to me?”

His face reddening, he says, “Not at all.”

“Where do you normally have lunch?”

“Cafeteria

“How about I meet you there?” I don’t feel like staying in this room the whole time.

“I’m not sure you can leave the room,” he says. “But I can ask.”

Excited at the prospect of leaving this room, I add, “It’d be nice to walk around a little.”

“Okay, I’ll be back around noon—when I go on break. Best case scenario, we’ll head over to the cafeteria together. Worst case scenario, you’ll have to endure my presence in your room for a little longer as I chow down on a turkey sandwich.”

“The horror!” I respond in mock outrage.

“I think you’re warming to my presence.”

“I wouldn’t say all that,” I deadpan.

“True. You didn’t bother using the number I took such a long time writing down after your mom asked,” he says and I laugh louder than I intended to at the reminder of my mom’s shamelessness.

I think he wanted me to call him—text him at least—and that makes me smile. “Maybe I’ll consider sending you a text this time.”

“Maybe you will,” he says. “And maybe I’ll consider having lunch elsewhere,” he jokes.

"That's fine by me," I retort. "It's not like I was the one asking." He walks out of the door, his laughter echoing down the hall.

I look around the room trying to find something to do. When my eyes land on the TV, I grab the remote connected to the bed and turn the channels until I find an episode of Gilmore Girls I've watched a million times before. Settling in with the blanket covering me, I give Rory and her drama my full attention.

Opening my eyes, I realize I fell asleep...and I'm still at the hospital. At least all the medical devices have been detached from my body and, in a way, I feel free.

"Oh, you're up," my mom says, walking into the room with a cup of coffee in hand and a smile on her face.

"How long have you been here for?" I ask. She's been getting better at not spending every single second of the day here. She may even start working part-time soon—if I can convince her to, that is.

"Only like an hour. I came in when you were already asleep. I watched some TV. I even read some gossip magazine in the waiting room—"

"I don't want to know which celebrity did what stupid thing, Mom," I tell her, knowing if I give her the chance she'll spend the next two hours chatting away.

"Fine, I'll keep it to myself... for now!"

"How long do I have to stay this time?" I ask, hoping it's not three days.

She closes the distance and pushes a strand of hair away from my face. "Dr. Roman said maybe two days this time," she says eagerly.

"Two days sounds better than three," Jesse says, coming to stand just inside the room.

"Mom, you remember Jesse," I tell her by way of reintroduction.

Turning to him she says, "How could I forget." But when she turns back to me, she winks.

"I just wanted to let you know you're good to hang at the cafeteria for a little while."

"You're going to the cafeteria?" Mom asks uncertainly.

I nod. "I'm having lunch with Jesse."

Her eyes light up and she looks from him to me a few times.

Crap.

"Not like that!" I yell.

"Not like what?" she asks, pretending not to know what I'm objecting to.

"Jesse just stopped by earlier and offered to have lunch with me," I tell her.

She looks at him. "Did he now?"

Jesse begins nervously tugging at his hair again. "I just thought Zoe would enjoy looking at a different set of walls," he reasons.

My mother smiles. "Such a thoughtful young man," she tells him. "So, what are you waiting for?"

"Do you want to go now or—wait? I'm okay either way," he replies, stumbling over his words. If this is how he acts around my mom, I can only imagine how nervous he'd be meeting my dad. Not that he has to—not that he ever will.

"Now's okay," my mom answers before I can. I give her a sidelong look and she lifts her shoulder as if asking '*what?*' Shaking my head, I slowly start lifting myself up from the bed, surprised when Jesse appears at my side a moment later.

Helping me, he asks, "You sure you want to get up?"

I see the concern in his eyes, but nod. "Yeah. I took a nap and everything. I need a break from this room." I take his hand and allow him to help me get up. The moment we touch, I feel a comforting feeling spread through my body. I almost pull out of his grasp, but think better of it. The last thing I want to do is fall face down on the floor—I think that'd be more embarrassing than my mom asking Jesse for his number.

"You good?" he asks when my feet touch the floor.

I nod. "Thanks." I let go of his hand and immediately miss the feeling from earlier.

"You're welcome to join us, ma'am," he says to my mother.

"I'll be okay," she replies with a mischievous gleam in her eye. "I've got a few errands to run. You two have fun."

She leaves the room and I look at Jesse and shrug. "Shall we?"

He nods. Out in the hallway, he clears his throat. "She scares me," he says.

"Who, my mom?" I ask, looking behind me as if she were there.

He nods again. "Yeah."

"She's harmless. She loves romance...hasn't got a filter though."

"Good to know," he says with a smile as we arrive at the cafeteria. He leads me to one of the tables closest to the door.

I take a seat, enjoying how normal this is. "She swears we've got a romance story waiting to be written." I don't know why I tell him that. Not only is it embarrassing, but it'll likely make things awkward and uncomfortable.

"I—"

"Don't worry. I've assured her there's nothing going on," I respond and he nods absentmindedly before walking over to the refrigerator. He hurries back to the table with a plastic bag in his hands and sits down. Opening it, he pulls out a zip-locked bag with a sandwich, chips, a green apple and a bottle of orange juice.

"Does your mom pack your lunches?" I ask, breaking the silence we've been sitting in for what feels like hours but has probably only been a few seconds.

He looks up at me. "Why do you ask?"

"Just seems really...healthy."

He opens the zip-locked bag and pulls out the sandwich. "We've got to watch what we eat—football rules and all." I nod in agreement like I know exactly where he's coming from.

He brings the sandwich to his mouth for a bite, but stops. "Do you want half?"

"You're asking me now?" I reply.

"Sorry. I didn't leave my house thinking I was going to have lunch with you. I didn't pack you anything."

"It's okay. I'm not hungry anyway. Chemo takes away my appetite."

He smiles apologetically. "Sorry." He digs further into the bag. "How about an apple?" he asks.

"I don't really want any food."

"You said okay to coming to lunch with me. The least you can do is eat," he says and I know he wants me to say yes to something so he can feel okay about eating too.

"You asked me, but whatever. I'll take the apple." He rolls the apple from his side of the table to mine. I grab it and take a bite. "An apple a day keeps the doctor away," he says with a rich laugh.

"Should have told me that earlier," I joke in response.

We spend the rest of his break talking about Bragan University and life in general. He tells me about how hard it's been to be an intern and then to show up at football practice and pretend he's not exhausted. I tell him more about Maria and some of the other patients on this floor. He asks me a few things about myself— like my favorite type of music and what I wanted to be when I grew up. The conversation flows smoothly—like two old friends catching up on all the things that have changed in each other's lives. When his break is up, he gives me his hand once again and guides me to my room.

"If you ever need a break from your room let me know," he says as we walk back.

"You going to give up your lunch breaks and spend them with me now?" I ask half-jokingly.

He slows his steps before responding, "I'd still eat, but you can sit in the cafeteria with me. It was nice getting to know more about you. I'll continue to bring you an apple if you join me," he says with a boyish smile and I laugh.

"I never thought I'd see the day where someone bribes me with an apple."

He lifts an eyebrow. "I never thought I'd do that either, but hey, there's a first time for everything."

We stand outside of my door, neither one of us ready to end whatever this is. "I'll join you again tomorrow, if that's okay," I reply cautiously.

"Of course that's okay. I was the one who asked," he says, following me inside the room.

I walk straight to my bed and, with little effort, take a seat. "It's nice of you to offer. Laying on the same bed for too many hours gets exhausting."

"I can't even imagine," he says, looking around the room.

His pager goes off breaking him from his thoughts, he looks down at it before speaking. "I've gotta go. If I can, I'll stop by later to check on how you're doing. Otherwise, I'll see you tomorrow for lunch."

"Don't forget my apple," I remind him.

"I wouldn't dare," he replies before walking out of the room.

9

JESSE

It's been a month since this internship started, and I'm surprised to find that I don't have to force myself to drive in the direction of the hospital anymore. I think Zoe has played a big part in that; being friends with her has made this place a little more bearable.

I knock gently on her open door, grinning when her face lights up.

"Ready to eat?" she asks, swinging her legs off the side of the bed.

I take her arm, steadying her. "Always," I say with a smile.

"You're starting to spend more time here than I do," she jokes.

"You did leave me here to fend for myself for days at a time," I reply. I'm glad she's gotten the chance to go home instead of being confined to this hospital, but I do miss seeing her whenever I want to.

"Are you admitting you're weak and need my help to get through this life?" she mocks.

I wink at her. "I'd never admit weakness."

"I'll take that as a yes then." She laughs and I join her.

"How are you doing?"

"I'm doing well. Doctor Roman says things are looking good," she says, putting the word 'good' in air quotes.

We reach the cafeteria and I rest my hand on the small of her back, ushering her through as I hold the door for us.

"You don't believe it?" I ask, breaking the contact. Damn, that had felt right.

She glances at me over her shoulder, her eyes blazing for a moment. "I'll believe it when I'm done," she says, and I can tell means it. She's a realist, but I know part of her wants to hope for more.

"You're almost done."

"Things could still go wrong," she whispers, taking a seat at our usual table.

I look at her—really look at her—before I speak. "Things can always go wrong." *Isn't that the truth?* I think bitterly. "But, they could also go right."

"When did you become such an optimist? That's not something I signed up for when I decided to be friends with you," she says, changing the subject.

I shrug. "Honestly, I don't know. And wait—are you saying we're friends now?"

"Maybe."

"Well, I'm going to get my lunch. When I get back, you can try that answer again."

Taking out my lunch, I turn back to the table to find her watching me.

"So?" I ask, sitting opposite her. "Are we friends or not?"

She folds her arms over her chest. "I guess," she says with theatrical reluctance.

I can feel the shit-eating grin stretching across my face. "Do you know what this feels like?" She shakes her head. "When the cool kid—the one you wanted to be friends with for a long time—finally says hello to you," I tell her and she rolls her eyes. I grab an apple from the lunch bag and hand it to her.

She takes a bite. "Are you saying I'm the cool kid you've looked up to your entire life?"

"Yes. Everyone here thinks you're the coolest." I know she doesn't believe it, but she's loved here—by the nurses, the other patients, and by the visitors. Even her sarcasm is something people admire. I've seen the way Dr. Roman talks about her, how Fiona smiles whenever she tells us a story about Zoe, and even personally when I've walked by Maria's room to find them all laughing at something Zoe has said or done. When I see her face redden, I add, "I had to figure out what people saw in you for myself."

"And what's the verdict?" she asks.

"You're okay, Evans."

She's more than okay. She's amazing.

"What is it with guys and last names?" she asks.

"Last names are reserved for friends," I respond. "None of my friends actually call me by my first name."

"Alright, then, *Falcon*. How's your day been?" she asks.

"Well, I ran around and got coffee—"

"As interns do," she adds and I smile.

I take a bite of the string cheese I grabbed from inside my lunch bag. "And then I shadowed Dr. Roman for a while."

"That sounds like a lot of learning,"

"I did learn a little, but there's so much more I don't know." The work this hospital does with its lack of resources is admirable and worthy of emulation.

"What else?" she pushes and I smile, happy she's interested in knowing more about me.

"I made Maria laugh by pretending to be a magician."

"A magician?" she repeats, her eyes widening.

"Yes, Jesse the Good Magician came out to play for a little."

"Why are you always the 'good' something?"

"Because I'm cool like that." I shake my head like she should know this and add, "The point is, I wanted to be a magician when I grew up and today I had the perfect opportunity to showcase my talents."

"I'm so mad I missed that," she says with a chuckle. "What made you change your mind?"

I laugh. "I grew up. Then I wanted to be a professional football player."

"So that's why you play football then? You want to do it professionally and have a career in medicine as a backup?"

"I don't want to play football professionally. Even if I did, it's almost impossible for kickers to get drafted."

"And the impossibility of it is what's stopping you? I thought you were an optimist!" she exclaims.

"I am an optimist." Most of the time.

"When did you decide you wanted to be a doctor?"

I was waiting for this question. I suck in a breath, praying she won't ask any follow-up questions. "High school."

"Why?"

"Just circumstances." It's a weak response—a half answer—because I don't want to discuss the topic of my motivation. Not right now. Not yet.

"Okay," she answers and I can tell she suspects there's more to the story.

"Any football games coming up?" she says, changing the topic.

"Not yet, but when we start playing, will you be cheering for me in the stands?"

She smirks, trying to suppress a laugh. "Nah, I'm good."

"Seriously?" I ask, pretending to be hurt that she wouldn't go watch me play.

"Well, maybe I'll cheer for you," she says, giving in. I laugh when I realize that had been her goal.

"I'll be looking for you in the bleachers."

"You won't find me."

"You're actually never going to go to one of my games?"

"I'll go, but with so many people there, you won't be able to see me."

"I'll see you," I assure her. I don't think anyone can miss her.

"Speaking of seeing, I've got to go," she says, getting up and tossing the core of the apple into the trash.

"Already?" I was hoping she could stay a little longer. "I'll see you at the same time tomorrow?"

She nods. "Same time tomorrow, until you get sick of it."

"I won't." I don't think I could get sick of seeing her.

She lifts an eyebrow and says, "You say that now."

"Don't make me change my mind," I warn.

She lowers her voice to a conspiratory whisper. "Think we'll be friends for long?"

"I hope we are."

The smile she gives me is hauntingly sad. "Have a good day, Falcon." She waves goodbye before walking out the door.

"You too, Evans," I respond. Tomorrow could not come fast enough.

10

ZOE

The following week, I return to the hospital for my scheduled chemo and three-day stay, but I'm told I won't be getting chemotherapy. Instead, Mom and I are ushered into one of the waiting rooms to wait for Dr. Roman. We both sit quietly, neither one of us saying anything—both consumed by fear.

A few minutes later, Dr. Roman walks in with my chart in hand. She greets us with a smile, sets the chart down, and takes one of the available seats in front of us.

"I have good news for you," she says. I look at my mother, who I can tell is ready to cry. Dad walks in at the same time Dr. Roman adds, "We're done with your chemo."

"What does that mean?" my father asks cautiously.

Dr. Roman turns to him. "It means that after looking at the results, we believe Zoe is now in remission." She turns back to focus on me. "We didn't find any cancer cells so we can say that the chemo has done its job."

"So, I'm good?" I ask. I'm waiting for her to take back the words I've waited months to hear.

"Yes, it seems the chemo was successful. We'll still need to see you every couple of weeks, but other than those check-ins, you're free to go back to normal life."

Normal life. I forgot what that was like, but as Dr. Roman says, I can have one again and I'm eager to start.

"And school?" I don't know why that's the first thing I ask but I do. Normal life included school for me, and although I haven't given it much thought, talking to Jesse about Bragan University has strengthened my desire to go back. My father clears his throat and when I turn toward him, I notice that my mother is standing beside him with her hand intertwined with his. She's got tears sliding down her face and my father looks surprised.

"Sweetie, thinking about school just yet isn't a great idea," Mom says jumping in before my dad says anything else.

"But, if I wanted to...could I go back?" I ask Dr. Roman once again, hoping she gives me the answer I want to hear.

"If that's something you want, yes. You could return to school," Dr. Roman confirms with a smile.

In what comes out like a whisper, I respond, "Thank you." Taking a deep breath, I add, "How soon could I return?" As I say this, I feel the hope I'd been so cautious about letting in before spread through my body.

"As soon as you'd like."

As soon as I want? What about right now? I don't ask those questions out loud.

"Shouldn't she stay home a little longer?" my father, a man of few words, asks, realizing I'm serious about going back. I know that he'll be the parent I have to target–the parent I'll have to plead to and convince. Although the ultimate decision is technically up to me, I need my parents on board too.

"You don't have to go back right away," Dr. Roman adds to appease my parents.

"I wouldn't. We're halfway through the summer, so there's a few months before the Fall semester starts," I inform her, but my comment is more for my parents. There's still time for them to coddle me, and time for me to make them see my point.

"Great! We'll keep an eye on you when you come in and hopefully things continue to go smoothly for you." I could read between the lines: I could relapse...just like Maria did.

The rest of the conversation and the questions my parents ask fall on deaf ears. I checked out the moment they started asking about the rules. Instead, I find myself thinking about the fact that I get to go back to school. I can return to Bragan University. I can be a student again. Sure, I won't get to be a senior this year, but I'll be a junior—and I'll be alive. The fact that I'll have to take a few extra classes to stay on track won't deter me either, or stop me from pushing forward.

Bragan University... I can't believe I'll get to start again in a few months.

I'm so eager to go that I don't mind all the things I hated when I was there: getting up early for class, or homework. Now, I'm looking forward to it.

Slowly, I retreat from the room, leaving my parents and Dr. Roman behind to find my own Good Doctor. Walking the halls of this hospital, I pass by Maria's room and peek inside only to find it empty. She's likely off getting some more invasive tests done and my heart immediately begins to ache at the thought that I'll be leaving when she has to stay.

I keep searching for Jesse, finally stopping at the cafeteria. When I scan the room, I spot the man I'm looking for sitting at one of the corner tables with Thing 1 and Thing 2—also known as Lilly and Marissa. I hear one of them giggle and see the other flip her hair as I approach. Jesse laughs at what one of them says, and in an instant, I change my mind. Why would Jesse care that I was officially in remission? I stop abruptly, and turn back towards the door.

"Hey, Zo!"

I glance over my shoulder to find Jesse grinning at me.

"I didn't see you come in," he says, standing up and walking over to me. The sour looks on the girls' faces is priceless, and I have to stop myself from smiling.

"I thought you'd be in the 'Poison Room'," he says, using air quotes on the last word.

"I thought I would be too. But I'm not," I answer cryptically.

"How come? Something wrong?" I'm pleased to see he's worried.

"Nope, nothing. I just wanted to grab some ginger ale," I lie. I don't know why I don't tell him the truth. It's not like we aren't friends.

"It's in the fridge."

"Yeah, I know," I answer, wishing I hadn't come in here in the first place. I head over to the fridge, grab a can of ginger ale, and open it. Slowly—carefully—I pour it into a plastic cup. Without looking at him again, I leave the cafeteria just as quickly as I walked towards it. I could've just told him—given him the news Dr. Roman gave me. Then again, if I say it out loud, I feel like I might jinx myself.

"Wait up," I hear him say behind me.

I look back, but don't slow my steps. "What's up?"

"You didn't go in there for ginger ale."

"Yes, I did."

"Jeez, Zoe, would you just stop?" he says, exasperated.

With a huff, I slow down enough for him to catch up. I show him my plastic cup. "See. Ginger ale."

"You didn't have to get it from the cafeteria," he says.

"What makes you say that?"

"Because there's a fridge closer to where you had your check- up."

He waits for me to contradict him, but he's caught me out. I shrug. "Do you regularly have lunch with the other interns?" I ask, jealousy rising in me.

He blinks, thrown by the change of subject. "Sometimes. I had to take an earlier break today, and I knew you had chemo." He starts running a hand through his hair.

"Are *you* okay?" I ask.

"I'll be fine," he says and I don't miss the fact that he's used the future tense.

He *will be* fine, but he's not right now.

"If you ever need to talk..." I mindlessly bring the rim of the cup to my lips.

"I thought you didn't like ginger ale anymore," he says.

"Yes, I do," I counter. I know he's changing the subject because he doesn't want to talk about himself. It's a classic deflecting technique.

"No, you said you stopped drinking it after you got to go home, remember? You told me you've had it too many times that you can only associate it with being in the hospital." I stare at him. We talked about that *weeks* ago; I can't believe he'd remember.

"Did I say that?" I say, feigning ignorance.

We stop near one of the nurse's stations. "You did. Now, tell me, why you came looking for me," he says this with a teasing smile.

"I did *not* come looking for you."

"No, you just came looking for the soda you don't like, in the cafeteria you knew I'd likely be in."

I give in. "Exactly."

He smiles more genuinely, making me smile as well. "What's up?" he asks.

"I just wanted to tell you I've been cleared. I don't have to come back every day anymore... I'm even allowed to go back to school." The words rush out of my mouth as I'm unable to contain the excitement. I swear Jesse's eyes light up—the shadows lurking there disappearing. Now all I see is joy and excitement. Unexpectedly, he lifts me up and spins me around.

"Stop!" I shout, laughing as the room spins around me. "You're spilling my drink."

"I'll clean it up later," he says, his laughter warming me. For a second, I enjoy this moment; I enjoy seeing him excited and the fact that I've gotten a second chance at life. I also find myself reveling in the way his hands feel against my skin.

"Put me down!" I tell him when I realize we're drawing an audience.

"Fine." When my feet finally touch the ground, he says, "That's amazing news, Zo."

"It is."

He's just staring at me now, and I can tell he's thinking about something. "Everything okay?" I ask once again.

"Yeah," he says and his hand goes to the back of his head. "I'm sorry about... you know, picking you up. I just... I'm really happy to hear you've been cleared."

I tentatively bring my hand to his shoulder to show him I didn't mind, I enjoyed it. "All good. I'm excited too!"

"So, you're going back to school?"

"Yes. Dr. Roman says I can go back to living a 'normal life' and that includes school."

"You're coming to Bragan?" he asks.

I nod. "I'll have to convince my parents, but yeah. If Bragan takes me back, I'll start in September."

"There's no way Bragan will say no to you. Your parents won't either. From what I've learned about you in the last few weeks, you're a hard person to say *no* to."

"Let's hope so. I think I can convince my parents, but B.U. could say no to letting me return."

"They'd better not. I'll have an entire football team sitting in their office if they do," he says with a wink.

"I'll let you know so you're ready to call for back-up."

"Would you be living on campus?" Jesse asks eagerly as I lead him in the direction of the front desk, where I know my parents are probably waiting for me.

"One step at a time, Doc. I've gotta get my parents—mostly my dad—on board with letting me re-enroll. Then I can drop the living-on-campus part."

I'm sure that's going to go well.

"I'll be living there too, remember. It'll be like having a doctor on call." I smile, but I can't help wonder if we'll still be friends when I start college. What if we return to school and he never talks to me again? I've gotten so used to having him around—so used to his friendship—that if it were to disappear, I don't know how I'd feel.

"Think you can talk to my parents for me?" I ask jokingly as I push away my thoughts.

"If I'm honest, I'd rather not. I can help you move in though, when the time comes," he says playfully bumping into me.

I shove him back. "Wuss."

"I can only imagine the things your dad would do to me."

"Stop! It's not a good image to have."

"And your mom? She scares me. If I were to show up at your house, I'm sure she'd think I was getting ready to ask you to marry me."

I chuckle nervously at the idea of marriage. "You're not wrong. It's probably better stay away from her otherwise she'll hunt you down and give you the ring herself." I'm babbling—I know I am—and I snap my mouth shut, trying to ignore the sudden tension in the air.

When we arrive at reception, I find my mom waiting. "Anyway, I've got to head home. I'll still have to come to the hospital twice a month, I think, and then it should be less once the semester starts."

"Text me if you need anything."

"I don't have your number."

"I gave it to you a while ago."

"I may have tossed it out," I lie. That piece of paper has been on top of my bureau, taunting me.

"Ouch," he says, his hand going to his chest as if I've wounded him. "Give me your phone."

I pretend to think about it. "Why?"

"I'm putting my number somewhere permanent," he says. Relenting, I pull my phone out of the back pocket of my jeans and hand it to him. He punches in a few numbers and then returns the device to me. When I look at the screen, I let out a loud laughter.

"'Good Doctor'? Really?" I ask, laughing at his choice of contact name.

"You've been calling me that for weeks already. It's time we make it official."

"I have not been calling you that. And you do know I can change it, right?"

"You won't," he says confidently.

"Want to try me?" I shoot back.

"I hope you don't." His tone is different now—unsure. "When's your next appointment?"

I clear my throat. "Two weeks from now, but I could be wrong. After Dr. Roman said I could go back to school, I stopped listening."

"Tsk. Tsk. Do you ever listen?"

"I take offense to that! I've been listening to your nonsense for weeks!"

"Don't act like you don't enjoy having me around." I do. More than he knows.

"You're okay, Falcon."

"You're okay too, Evans."

11

ZOE

"So, you're moving into which dorm again?" Jesse asks, sitting next to me in the hospital's cafeteria.

"I'm moving into the one by the quad. New Dorm?"

He hands me an apple and grabs another for himself. "You're aware it's not called New Dorm, right?"

"What's it called then?" When I'd started college a few years ago, the dorm had been newly built. The students took to naming it New Dorm, and by the time someone made a large enough donation to get their name on the front, we'd already gotten used to calling it by its nickname. "See, you don't even know!" I mock when he doesn't answer.

"You're right. I don't know," he says laughing. "The incoming students will call it by its new name. Too late to fix the rest of us," he reasons with a smile.

"I thought it was never too late to fix things, Mr. Optimist."

His eyes connect with mine before he says, "Most things can be fixed, some things can't."

"Anyway, if you're going to continue being my friend you're going to have to accept the fact that I'm never wrong." I point at his chest. "Anything—and everything—I say, is gospel," I tell him pointing.

"Really? Is that so?" he questions, his hand inching closer to my own on the table. I look directly at it, willing him to touch me.

"Yes, sir," I respond when I realize he's waiting for me to answer.

"We'll see."

I take a bite of my apple. "Where are Thing 1 and Thing 2?" I cover my mouth when I realize I've said that out loud.

"Who are Things 1 and 2?" he asks.

"The two other interns."

He grins. "Jeez, what did they do to earn those nicknames?"

I shrug. "I don't know which one is which."

"Lilly is the blonde; Marissa is the brunette," he explains. "I think," he adds, and I laugh.

"You don't know which one is which either!" I celebrate silently the fact that I'm not the only one that can't tell them apart. Or that's what I tell myself. Really, I'm celebrating knowing that he hasn't paid enough attention to tell them apart. Inside of me, the little girl with the silly school girl crush jumps up and down in excitement.

"I don't know where they are—and I don't really care. When do you move in? That's what's more important," he says making my cheeks heat.

"When does everyone move in?" I ask sarcastically.

"You really are a smartass. You do know that, right? When I first met you, I thought you were going to be nice." He throws his finished apple into the trashcan and looks back at me. "Boy, was I wrong."

"When I first met you, I thought you were too young and good-looking to be a doctor."

Shit!

Did I just say that out loud?

"I guess we were both wrong," I add as a punchline.

"You're killing me, Evans. I'm not a doctor yet, but the *young- and-good-looking* thing? You're right on the money," he says with a wink.

I laugh. "Nah, I was wrong about those things too."

"You don't think I'm young?"

"Okay," I concede. "I was right about you being young."

"Oh, so it's just the good-looking part you have an issue with? Am I not handsome enough for you, Evans?" he asks.

Clearing my throat, I say, "You're okay-looking." I take another bite of my apple. "You were wrong about me too."

"I know; you're not nice."

"Nope, I'm a tough cookie. Some would even describe me as heartless."

"So, to prove you're mean, you compare yourself to a cookie? Way to go, Evans." He pauses, thinking for a moment before adding, "I think you're nice, but I also think you're a lot more than that."

"A lot more?" I say, suddenly breathless.

"You're fiery, energetic, rebellious, funny, and a definite pain in my ass!" He laughs. "I bet you could make a grown man cry if you wanted to."

"What makes you say that?"

"Just a hunch." His gaze is fixed on me, and I fidget uncomfortably in my seat. With a lazy grin, he says, "So, you're moving in the weekend everyone else does?"

"Yep."

"Do you need some help? I'm available."

"I'm moving into a dorm the size of a box. I don't think I'll have much to carry so I'll pass on the help. My parents are coming anyway...but I appreciate the offer."

"Are you sure?"

I smile at his eagerness. "I think my parents and I can handle a few boxes. Thanks."

"Are you sure you want to miss out on seeing this young, good-looking doctor lifting boxes and breaking a sweat?" he asks, flexing his arms. I stare unashamedly at his incredible muscles, then let out a raucous laugh.

"I think I'll survive."

He shrugs. "Your loss, Evans."

"I'll recover, Falcon."

"Hey...ah..." He plays with invisible lint on his scrubs. "Do you think you'll still want to be friends with me when you go back to college?" he asks and I can hear the vulnerability in his voice.

"God, no," I say with a wide smile. "I can't wait to get rid of you. I've had to deal with you here for almost the whole summer. I don't think I can take any more."

He chuckles. "I'm literally the best thing to have happen to you this summer. Don't pretend it isn't true."

"I don't know about all that," I tell him but his words hold some truth. He *is* one of the best things to come out of this summer. He's helped me forget about my day-to-day battles, to look forward to the moment he walks through my door to say hello.

"You know I have been," he coaxes. "Don't deny it."

Begrudgingly, I say, "You haven't been the worst thing to happen to me this summer."

I'm grateful he still wants to stay in touch—be friends with me—even after all this is in the past.

He takes in a dramatic breath and blows it out. "Phew, I was beginning to worry that you were going to shut down my friendship offer."

"When you say things like that it makes me want to reconsider," I joke.

"Seriously though, I feel like I barely see you anymore."

"That's because I'm not here all the time, and I'll be here less and less."

"Three to four times a month from now on, right?"

I dangle the core of my apple between my fingers. "Something like that."

"See, that's why we've gotta start... hanging out outside of this place. Maybe a cafeteria out in the world somewhere?"

"My parents are very cautious and don't want me hanging outside too often," I tell him honestly.

"Well, maybe one day we can hang out in your living room."

"Maybe. You'll have to endure my parents though."

"For the sake of our friendship, I'll make the sacrifice."

"Cool."

"We can also hang out when school starts too."

"I haven't even started school and you're already making plans for us?"

"You're going to be swarmed with guys the moment you step on campus. I just want to make sure I get ahead of the masses."

I stare at him and he shrugs. "That's not going to happen. And in an alternate universe where that's even a possibility, I'd still make room for you on my calendar," I tell him.

"That's all I ask."

I nod. "I can give you that."

12

ZOE

I spend the whole day running—well, more like walking—around my room, picking up all the clothes I've left on the floor and repositioning anything that might be out of place. Jesse's coming over to hang out today and I'm terrified. I told Mom last night and, together, we told Dad. A wordless conversation ensued, with him giving us raised eyebrows and a million unspoken questions, but when Mom gave him a long look of consternation, he conceded.

Ding dong.

"Door!" Mom yells from the kitchen.

Like I didn't hear the bell myself?

Nervous beyond belief, I take slow measured steps into the living room and open the door.

"Hey," Jesse says. But I don't respond—I can't. I look him up and down, mute. It's the first time I've seen him without scrubs. He's wearing jeans and a t-shirt—nothing too extravagant, but they complement his body.

I look back up to find him watching me.

"You're not wearing scrubs," I tell him.

"I don't think I'm allowed to wear them on off days," he says with a teasing smile.

I shake my head. *Idiot*. "Come in," I tell him, taking a step back.

As soon as he's inside, I shut the door and let out a breath.

"Come on," I say, leading him to my room. Mom said it would be fine for us to hang up there as long as the door was left open.

We enter my room and he takes a seat on my reading chair while I sit on my bed. The room is as clean as it's ever been and I internally high-five myself.

We sit in silence for a few minutes before Jesse says, "Tell me a little more about you, Red." He stretches out his long legs looking, oddly enough, like he's been coming here forever.

"I'm Red now? I thought we were on a last name basis," I say, shifting around on my bed.

"You need to have more than one nickname."

"What for?"

He grins. "One is never enough."

"I guess two nicknames is fine, but at least make one of them original," I joke.

"Do other people call you Red?" he asks, feigning shock. "You mean my nickname for you isn't unique?"

"Is the sky blue?" I wait for the smile I know is going to appear on his face, and like clockwork, he gives it to me.

Mom knocks on my already open door and walks in. "I've brought cookies and milk," she announces, gesturing to the platter in her hand. A chocolaty smell invades every inch of the room, making my mouth water.

"You didn't have to, Mrs. Evans," Jesse tells my mother as she places the cookies and milk on the nightstand between us.

"I've got to feed you to keep you coming back," she responds and I give her the look that will hopefully get her to stop embarrassing me. The woman is on a mission—and once she sets her mind on something, it's hard to get her to give her up. The phrase 'a dog with a bone' could not be a more apt description of my mom.

Jesse blushes. "I'll keep coming as long as Zoe wants me here," he says, and I swear my mother smiles as he's given *her* the biggest compliment of her life.

She pats him on the shoulder. "You can come over whenever you want. Will you stay for dinner, sweetheart?" she adds. I look to the window, finding the sun setting.

How long have we been talking?

"I'd love to," he answers at the same time I say, "I'm sure he has better things to do, Mom."

"See, Z, he doesn't have anything better to do than spend time with you."

Take me now, I silently beg. *Rescue me from the mortification of sitting here and listening to my mother.*

Jesse grabs a chocolate chip cookie from the nightstand and stuffs it in his mouth.

"This is delicious," he exclaims, covering his mouth with his hand.

"Good, but don't eat too many. You don't want to spoil your appetite," my mother says, placing a kiss on my forehead and patting Jesse's shoulder once again on her way out. I'm surprised when she closes the door fully behind her.

Jesse moans in utter bliss after stuffing another cookie in his mouth. "Mmm, so good."

I feel a blush color my cheeks. I don't even want to begin to explore what that sound does to me.

"Good?" I ask a little out of breath.

He swipes his tongue over his bottom lip to catch a stray crumb. "Amazing."

I need to distract myself from looking at his mouth. Clearing my throat, I ask, "So, can I have a different new nickname?"

"Firecracker, Fire, Spitfire, Furnace," he suggests, listing them on his fingers.

I grab a cookie. "Those are literally all red-themed. I get it; I'm a redhead."

"You're the second redhead I know, and the other one I call by his last name."

"So just keep calling me by mine and we can forget about the second nickname. I don't have a second one for you."

"You could come up with one."

I take a bite of my cookie, chewing slowly before saying, "That's a lot of work."

"Fine. I'll just call you Evans... for now."

"You could even call me Zoe," I say trying to avoid the nicknames altogether.

He shakes his head. "Nope, just Evans."

"Fine."

He grins. "Fine. What do you do for fun now that you're at home?" he asks, grabbing one of the glasses of milk from the nightstand and taking a sip.

I reposition myself on the bed, resting back against the headboard. "You mean while my parents loom over my shoulder?"

"Beats being at the hospital," he responds quickly.

"I thought you liked hospitals, *Doctor* Jesse."

His expression becomes guarded. "Not particularly."

"Why not?" I press. I feel like I might be overstepping our friendship, but I won't back down.

"I mean, does anyone like hospitals—*really* like them?" he asks rhetorically. "People don't go there because it's fun. They go there because they're sick, or to see someone who's sick..." He takes a deep breath. "Doctors go there to serve. Patients go there seeking help," he finishes and I mull over his words.

"I agree." That's all I add to his statement because every word he's uttered is true. "Speaking of the hospital, how do you like your internship so far?" I ask.

"It's Saturday, and my day off. Do we have to talk about it?"

"That bad?" I ask.

"Not really. Just Things 1 and 2 need a lot of help figuring things out."

"Stealing my nickname for them, I see," I say, only a little smugly. "And of course they need *your* help."

"I've grown to like it. And why do you say it like that?" he asks, taking yet another cookie.

"Isn't it obvious? They both like you."

"Sure they do," he says in disbelief.

"They do. Like actually *like* you. That's why they follow you around like lost puppies."

"Oh jeez," he says, and I smile because I can see in his face that the thought of them liking him doesn't please him.

"How long until the internship finishes?"

"About two weeks." He looks relieved at the thought and I completely understand. He's been doing the internship along with football practices and scrimmages. I know he's exhausted. I still can't believe he made time to come hang out with me.

"And then I won't see you again?" I say out loud, more a statement than a question.

"Wrong. We'll be going to the same school, remember? I expect to see you more than I do now when my internship is over." His words make me smile like an idiot.

I wink. "Hmm, we'll see."

"Don't forget about our friendship just because you'll be back in college."

"Don't forget about me just because you'll be a senior and I'm just a measly junior," I remind him. He's at the top of the food chain being a football player and all. I have to remind myself that this—us—is only supposed to be temporary. We became friends out of convenience over the summer and the summer is almost gone. Once school starts, I don't know what'll happen.

"I wouldn't dare forget about you, Evans," he says, and I realize how much those words mean. Not because they're coming from him, but because other people have forgotten about me and the reassurance that someone else won't comforts me. "Back to the original question: what do you do for fun here?" He takes a bite of the cookie he's been holding, and I watch his reaction, unable to stop myself from zeroing in on the way he licks his lips afterwards. He looks back at me with his baby-blue eyes and I realize he's waiting for me to answer.

"I watch Friends," I blurt out.

"Let's watch it until dinner's ready," he says excitedly.

My eyes widen. "Are you a fan?"

"If you repeat that outside of this room, I will deny it."

I make the scout's honor sign. "I won't repeat it."

"Get to it, Evans!" he urges me.

"You're bossy. I may have to rethink my promise of keeping your secret obsession."

"You're playing a dangerous game," he jokes.

As I turn on the TV and scroll through my purchase list for Friends, I can't help but think that this is a dangerous game I'm playing, but one I don't want to stop.

13

JESSE

"What are you doing this weekend?" I ask Zoe, nervously. I don't want to come off too intense—too needy.

"Nothing much. Same thing I do every day," she answers from her place on the hospital bed.

"Home, bed, and Friends?" I ask, surprising myself with how well I know her already.

"Nah, I'm going skydiving," she responds sarcastically, and I smile at her smartass reply.

Her mother chooses that moment to walk into the room and I can't believe that regardless of how many times I've seen her, even in her own house, I can't help but be terrified of her.

With a smile on her face, Mrs. Evans greets me. "Hi, Jesse."

"Hi, Mrs. Evans," I respond.

"It's nice to see you," she says, patting my shoulder.

"It's nice seeing you too," I answer, doing my best to swallow my nerves.

"I overheard you asking Zo what she's doing this weekend," she says.

"Ah, yes." *Great! She probably thinks I want to ask her daughter on a date or something.*

I quickly glance at Zoe to find her cheeks reddening, her eyes fixed on her mother, waiting to see what she'll say next.

"How's the internship going?" Zoe blurts out. It's a question she already knows the answer to so I assume it's to distract her mother.

My eyes dart between Zo and her mom. "Umm...it's going pretty well—ending in a couple weeks." I can't wait to get a break from this place.

"I'm sure they'll miss having you around here," she finishes, and for a brief moment, I think she's going to say something else.

I wished she'd said something else.

"I'll miss everyone too. I'll come and visit though. And I'll get to see you at school."

My pager, which shouldn't belong in this century, goes off. With a shrug, I say, "Duty calls."

"I'll see you around," she says and her mother gives her a wide-eyed stare.

"What?" Zoe hisses at her.

"Ask him!" her mother whispers back.

I bite my cheek to stop myself from laughing out loud. "Ask me what?" I ask, ignoring the constant buzzing on my hip.

"About this weekend," Zoe's mom replies.

Zoe looks to me and then back at her mom. "It's not that important," she tells her in a low, agitated voice.

"Yes, it is," her mom argues.

"You ladies do know I'm still here, right? I can hear everything you're saying."

Zoe and Mrs. Evans turn to me, both of them looking slightly embarrassed.

Placing both hands on her hips, Mrs. Evans says, "Tell him."

"Yes, tell me!" I insist.

With a resigned breath, Zoe says, "My birthday is this weekend,"

"What? That's awesome!"

"We're having a party," her mother jumps in, unable to contain her excitement. I don't blame her. A few months ago, I bet she was wondering if she'd see her daughter live to see the next year of her life.

"It's not really a party," Zoe hedges.

I bite back a smile. "Will there be a birthday cake?"

"Yeah," she answers, her eyes bouncing around the room.

"Sounds like a party to me! How come you haven't invited me?"

"I didn't think you'd want to come," she says, shifting her gaze from me to the floor.

"Are you kidding me? I'd love to come."

"It's nothing serious—not like a real party or anything. It'll only be my parents, a few of their friends, and me. Dad will be barbecuing."

"You had me at cake, but the barbecue just sweetened the deal. I'll be there."

She smiles weakly. "Great. I'll text you the details," she responds just as my pager pings again.

"I can't wait," I tell her. "But look, I've gotta go and see what Fiona needs. I'll talk to you later?"

I wait for her nod before hauling ass out the door.

"Slow down, Falcon," Nick complains when I bump into him as I rush into the locker room.

"I got places to be!" I shout, stripping down to hit the showers.

"Oh really, Lover Boy? Have you found yourself a lady we don't know about?" Zack jokes, and I shake my head. These guys just don't know when to stop.

I walk over to the showers with Zack and Nick right behind me. "Wouldn't you like to know?" I tease because I'm in a good mood and if practicing in this heat didn't ruin it, nothing else will.

"Seriously though, why the rush?" Nick asks.

"I have a birthday party to attend," I answer and immediately regret it.

I let the water run over my head as I wash away the sweat from today's practice. "You have a party to go to and you're not inviting us?" Zack asks, pretending to be hurt.

I wrap the towel around myself and exit the showers. "Exactly," I reply. Once again, the duo follows right behind me as I walk into the locker room and start getting dressed.

"Why you gotta be like that man? We want to party too," Zack whines.

"You party every day, dude."

"So?" Nick says like that's no big deal.

I pull on my shirt. "This is for a hospital patient," I tell them, hoping it gets them off my case.

"Oh, never mind then," Nick says, immediately backing off.

"I'm all good," Zack responds.

"Really? You guys don't want to come?" I add, just because seeing them scram is entertaining.

"Nah, I just remembered I've got some homework to catch up on," Zack says, and while I want to say that's a bullshit excuse, he probably does have homework. He's been taking summer classes in addition to football practice, and whatever the hell else he does almost every night.

Putting on my pants and shoes, I grab my gym bag and stuff all the gear inside. I tell the guys that I'll see them later and zoom out of the locker room.

I take hurried steps over to my car because I'm eager to see Zoe, to spend her birthday with her. I reach my car, throw the gym bag into the trunk, and get into the driver's seat.

The drive to Zoe's house only takes me a few minutes. Parking my car on the side of the street, I grab the flowers, balloons, and chocolate I'd bought for her birthday gift. I don't know if she's the kind of girl that likes flowers, balloons, or chocolate, so I got all three just to be safe. For some reason, not knowing what she likes or dislikes bothers me, and I make a mental note to get to know her better.

With all three gifts in my hand, I make my way to her front door. Unlike earlier, my steps aren't rushed, instead, I walk slowly and I know it's because I'm nervous. This is a special day for her and I don't know whether I should be here, whether she wants me here. All I know is that this is where I want to be—I've been looking forward to it all week.

ZOE

"I GOT IT," I YELL THE MOMENT I HEAR THE DOORBELL RING. I TAKE THE stairs down two at a time excited about who's likely waiting on the other side.

"Slow down," my father yells from the kitchen and I watch him grab more meat from the fridge before retreating to the backyard where he's been grilling for the last two hours. How did he even know I was running? I guess parents do know everything.

I take a moment to catch my breath, then I pry the door open. I'm met by giant balloons and a bouquet of roses. Behind them is a very tall, handsome dark-haired guy.

"Happy birthday, Red," he says with the biggest smile, and I can't help but smile back.

"I thought we got rid of 'Red'," I counter.

He chuckles. "Happy birthday, Evans," he corrects.

"Thank you, Doc." We stare at each other for a few seconds, both too caught up taking each other in.

"You look..." He stops mid-sentence. "...beautiful."

I blush. "Thanks. You look great too."

"Don't lie to me, Evans. I came here straight from practice."

"In that case, you stink."

"I showered!" he argues and I laugh.

"Fine, you smell okay," I tease. "Come in," I say, taking a step back.

He hands the balloons to me and sets down the flowers and what

I think is a box of chocolates on the table closest to the door. "I smell freaking great," he says, and to prove his point, he envelops me in a huge bear hug. I breathe him, confirming what I already know: he smells amazing, like comfort...like home.

"Thanks," he replies, and that's when I realize I said all that out loud.

Shit!

"You should really keep your internal monologue... internal."

"It's my birthday, so forget I said anything," I reply, my face likely beet red.

"I don't think I'm ever going to forget you telling me I smell amazing... like home," He adds, his arms still wrapped tightly around me.

I feel goosebumps spread over my body the longer we stand like this—the longer I'm in his arms. "We're still hugging me, you know?"

"I... I know," he says making no effort to let go.

I feel the air around us change—a different feeling, one I can't describe. I'm afraid to think about it too hard though. "Err, you can let go now," I reply, trying to push out of his embrace.

"What? Don't want to keep inhaling my manly cologne?"

"You're too much!"

With a chuckle, he releases me and I take a step backwards. Immediately, I miss the closeness of his body.

"I'm just enough," he answers and I shake my head.

I paraphrase the quote from one of my favorite movies and say, "You're killing me, Falcon,"

His blue eyes focus on mine. "You're saving me, Evans."

14

ZOE

It's a couple of weeks before the end of the summer, and my parents and I go to see Dr. Roman again. We've been going to the hospital every few weeks as instructed, but we had one more visit—the most important visit, the one that would confirm I could return to school in the Fall.

Dr. Roman smiles at us as she walks into the room we've all been anxiously waiting in.

"How are you, Zoe? Feeling well?" she asks.

I nod, too frightened to speak.

"She's been just fine," my mom says, answering for me like I'm a little girl again.

The doctor looks at my parents briefly before fixing her attention on me. "I have some news, Zoe."

Her words make me take in a deep breath, and my mom reaches out to grasp my hand, squeezing it tightly.

"You're in complete remission."

For a moment, nobody says anything, the silence only broken by my mom's unrestrained sob. I look over at her, seeing the tears glistening on her cheeks. My dad has his arm wrapped around her, his eyes also red. Despite the tears, I can see their happiness, can sense the weight that's lifted from their shoulders. They've been given a second chance...we all have.

"I know you're excited, Zoe," Dr. Roman says, "but you need to be aware that a relapse is always a possibility."

I nod again, the ability to speak not quite returning yet. I swallow and force the words out. "But I don't need any more chemotherapy, right?"

"Right," she replies with a smile. "And you could even think about returning to school if that was something you wanted to do."

"We can talk about that later," my dad says, dismissing the idea altogether.

Pressing my lips together, I say to Dr. Roman, "Thank you... for everything."

She stands up, straightening her white coat. "I'm not the one who did the fighting." Reaching out, she squeezes my hand comfortingly. "Go home. Enjoy this moment with your parents." Leaning in, she adds in a conspiratory whisper, "Broach the topic of school when they're relaxed. Have a decisive plan and stick to your guns, Zo. You got this."

I WAIT A WEEK BEFORE HAVING THE CONVERSATION WITH MY PARENTS. I'd run through all the possible ways I could get them to come around to the idea of letting me move out and start living my life—the life I almost lost to cancer. Jesse helped me come up with a plan, and tonight is the night I tell them. Classes are about to start and I don't want to miss yet another first day.

I walk downstairs, moving in the direction of the sound of the TV. I step into the room, clearing my throat.

"Hey sweetie," my father says.

Deep breath, Zoe. "Can I talk to you guys for a few minutes?" I ask, my voice breaking.

"Is everything okay?" my mom asks as Dad mutes the television.

"Yes, everything's good. I just..." I pause and take a seat on the adjacent couch. I straighten my spine, trying to exude the courage I've work so hard to build this past week. "I want to go back to school this semester."

"*This* semester?" my mother asks.

I nod. "School is about to start. I don't want to lose another year."

"Zoe," my father interjects. "I think we should be cautious and wait a little longer."

"I've waited long enough," I fire back.

He stares at me before saying, "Okay. Well, your mom and I will talk about it more. Maybe you can ease into it by taking a couple of classes this semester?"

"I want to live on campus," I add, even though I know they'll say no. I just hope I can persuade them to change their minds.

Mom sits down next to me. "I don't think it's time yet," she says.

I know she's fighting this because she doesn't want to let me out of her sight. When I was diagnosed, she left her job and made taking care of me her first and only priority.

I take her hand in my own. "I do, Mom. I want to. I'm ready."

Brushing some hair behind my ear, she says, "We can talk about it later. Let your dad and I discuss it more."

I look at my dad, who is still sitting on the couch to my right with a puzzled look on his face. "Dad, I really need to go back."

"Why now? Why not wait a little longer?"

"So much time has gone by already. I don't want to wait anymore."

"Sweetie, the doctor just cleared you. I think it makes sense to—" Mom chimes in from next to me.

Before she can continue though, I say, "Mom, I know it's hard, but it's something I really want to do. Please understand where I'm coming from."

"Your dad and I will talk about it and then we'll discuss this again," she says, effectively tabling the topic. Despite their protests, I know this is progress.

"Want to watch this movie with us?" my dad asks, happy to change the subject.

"Sure," I tell him.

I know I'll get them to say yes. I need this. I'm confident I can get Mom on side—it's dad I have to worry about.

We join dad on the couch and I watch the movie, but my mind isn't registering what's actually happening. Instead, I'm thinking about what it will be like to return to Bragan—to be a student again.

I CAN'T BELIEVE TODAY IS THE DAY I MOVE INTO MY DORM ROOM. My parents and I spoke with the admissions office and they immediately approved my return to school. I'm sure my parents were hoping for a different answer, but it's time.

My mom lingers in my room, finally asking the question I know she's been mulling over this whole time. "Are you sure you're going to be okay here… alone?"

"Honey, it's time," my dad says, carrying in the last box into the room and shutting the door behind him. Oddly enough, convincing my dad hadn't been the hardest part—it was my mom. Then again, she did quit her job to care for me so the thought of not seeing me every day is probably hitting her harder.

I try to reassure her with a smile. "Mom, I'll be okay. I'm a short drive from home."

"Remember that if you need something, *call me*. And if you feel even slightly unwell, call 911 and then call me."

"I know the drill, momma. This isn't the first time you've dropped me off," I remind her, kissing her on the cheek.

She looks at me adoringly. "This time is harder than the last."

"Let's hope this time is better than the last. I'm only a ten-minute drive away," I tell her, smiling yet still holding back tears. The truth is, I'm scared too, but I won't admit that. It's hard enough already.

"You could always live at home and take classes on campus?" she insists.

"The doctors said this would be okay. Dr. Roman said the treatment's working and that I should be fine. She said I can live a normal life, Mom. *This* is part of me living a normal life."

Ignoring me, she says—almost desperately, "Robert, I don't think she's ready to be on her own yet."

My father's rests his hands on her shoulders and says, "Dani, I don't want her to stay here either, but we have to let her make her own choices."

"Yes, you do!" I chime in. "I stayed home for a full year of college. I want the full experience so I've got to submerge myself in it, dorm living and all."

"Not the *full* college experience," my dad corrects.

I smile at them innocently. "Most of the typical college experiences."

"Some," my dad fires back, causing my mom to smile and shake her head.

The smile soon falters though. "Are you sure you'll be okay, Zo?"

"Yes, Mom. I'm done letting illness control my life. And if something comes up, I know what to do. Cancer has taken too much away from me; I don't want to let it take any more."

My mother tears up as she moves towards me with open arms. "You are so strong, sweetheart."

I hug her back tightly. "You've taught me that, Mom—you and Dad. We've been fighting for my life for a year now. It's time I get to live it, don't you think?" I ask, discreetly wiping away the tears sliding down my face.

"Yes, it is. You fought and kicked cancer's ass. College will be a walk in the park in comparison."

I pull out of my mother's embrace and wipe away her tears. "Okay, enough with the crying," I tell them.

"Danielle, it's time to go."

My mother takes a deep breath. "Fine," she says, giving me one more hug before standing next to my dad.

"See you for Sunday lunches?" Dad asks, but I know it's more of an expectation.

"Always, Dad."

"You can bring Jesse too if you'd like?" my mother says with a devious smile. I could see my father visibly stiffen next to her.

"I'll think about it," I reply with a smile.

"Call me every day," Mom adds before twisting the knob on the door.

I smile coyly. "I will, and I'll tell you all about the boys I meet and the parties I go to."

"Zoe Evans," my dad says sternly.

My mom smiles. "Very funny," she says. I walk over to where they both stand and give them each a hug goodbye then close the door behind them. I know today is very emotional for all of us, but I think in a weird way it's also a relief. I mean, we're all going back to a normal routine.

I'm here.

I'm alive.

I'm a normal college student. There's got to be some joy in that.

School isn't a place I saw myself going back to, and while I know my parents hoped I would, they didn't know either. This step? It's monumental for us, despite the fact that it scares the hell out of me.

I *will* be okay though.

I look out the window and see the quad right below me. There are students sitting on the grass with books in their hands. At the other end, I count a group of five students playing Frisbee, tossing it back and forth and laughing. Students are everywhere—just like I remember—except this time, I taking it all in. I'm stopping to smell the roses, as they say, because I didn't know what I had until it was ripped away from me.

I grab my cell phone from the study table at my end of the room and type out a quick message to Jesse letting him know I'm here.

Jesse: This place just got a lot better.

I GRIN LIKE AN IDIOT.

This year is going to be great.

Bragan University, I'm back.

15

ZOE

The distinct sound of jingling keys followed by the twisting and turning of a doorknob causes me to open my eyes and sit up immediately. I look around for my phone, my eyes adjusting to the light coming from the window.

The keys rattle a little more before the door bursts open and a blonde girl wearing glasses walks in.

"I'm so sorry!" the girl exclaims, dragging in a suitcase after her.

Pulling my blanket towards me, I ask, "Can I help you?"

"Uh, I don't think so," she responds, looking around the room. I clutch the blanket a little closer, wondering why there's someone in my room this early in the morning.

"My name's Emma," she says, extending her hand to me.

I blink, immobile for a moment. "Hi, Emma. I'm Zoe," I say, shaking her hand cautiously.

When I realize she isn't going to let go of my hand, I pull mine back. "Crap, I—sorry," she says, finally looking chagrinned. "I probably should've started by saying I'm your roommate. Sorry if I woke you up."

Of course she's my roommate! I think. *Why else would she have a key?* "No worries. I should've already been up by now," I say, yawning. I'm surprised I slept this much. I was prepared to have a sleepless night, being in a new place and all, but I guess I was wrong.

"Are you a freshman?" I ask, hoping she isn't. Freshmen tend to be kids whose biggest worry is how they can become popular and I'm not up for that.

She pushes her glasses up a little higher on her nose. "No, actually. I'm a Junior."

"Great, me too!" I say, relieved. "So why are you switching dorms your junior year?"

"I had a few issues with my previous roommate and decided it was time to switch it up."

My eyes widen. I really hope she isn't going to be problematic.

"Oh no! Not like that! *My roommate* was the problem not me," she says.

"Okay." Though I'm not sure I believe her. I mean why would she admit to being the problematic one to a new roommate?

"I know you have no reason to believe me, but my old roommate was a bit of a bully," she adds, readjusting her glasses once again.

"Remind me never to play poker," I mutter under my breath.

"What?"

"Nothing," I say. "I'm sorry you had to deal with that."

"Don't worry about it. Hey, so I'll be coming in and out of the room to move my things in today. I'm basically just walking them from one building to the other so it'll probably take me the whole day. Sorry I woke you up, but I don't know how much sleep you'll get with me settling in today," she says without pausing to take a breath.

"Do you need any help?" I ask.

"No, I'm okay," she replies, sitting down on her unmade bed. I have a feeling she'd like the help but is the type of person who doesn't want to feel like she's bothering anyone.

"I can help," I insist, a little surprised I'm so willing to help out a stranger. Then again, we'll be sharing this room so we might as well start off on the right foot.

"Are you sure?"

I look at her—*really* look at her. She's very pretty—tall with long blonde hair that cascades over her shoulders.

I push the blanket down and get up. "Yeah, I'm sure. Just give me a few minutes to brush my teeth and throw on some clothes."

"You're a saint! I'll do another trip while you get ready," she says, already walking towards the door.

"I'll be ready in five if you want to just wait for me?"

"Sounds good! I left another box downstairs with the RA. I'll go grab it and then I'll be back in a jiffy."

A jiffy? *Interesting choice of words.*

"Great," I answer just as she walks out the door.

I head to the bathroom to brush my teeth and run the hairbrush through my hair. It isn't anywhere as long as what it was before the cancer, but it's growing. Sweeping it up, I secure it into a ponytail, change into shorts and a t-shirt then exit the bathroom.

As I sit down to wait for Emma to return, my phone starts to ring.

I search all over my bed until I find it wrapped inside my blanket. I press the center button and see Jesse's name and an incoming text.

Jesse: I have practice today but we should grab food after. Sorry I couldn't meet you yesterday!

He practices a lot from what I can tell. Last night he apologized for not coming to welcome me. He'd had an out-of-town scrimmage with another team.

Me: I'll think about it… My new roommate is moving in today and I might try and do something with her.

Jesse: Already replacing me, I see?

I smile.

Me: Not yet, Falcon. I'll see if she wants to do something and let you know.

Jesse: I'll be waiting.

I find myself re-reading his message a few times but before I can respond, I hear the doorknob jiggle again and I get up to open it for Emma. She's balancing a giant box in one hand and holding the keys with the other.

"I can help with that," I tell her, grabbing the box and awkwardly setting it down on top of the vacant bed next to my own. "Jeez, what have you got in there?" I ask, shaking out my arms.

"Books!" she beams. "And thank you."

"Are you ready to go?"

"Let's get this over with," she says with a chuckle.

JESSE

I PUT MY PHONE IN MY POCKET WHEN I REALIZE I'M NOT GETTING A response. Typical Zoe—always keeping me on my toes. I couldn't help her move in yesterday because we had an away pre-season game and by the time we got back, it was too late. Plus, the guys wanted to celebrate—and I couldn't back out.

I guess it makes sense that she wants to get to know her roommate, but I can't help wanting her to spend time with me. I haven't seen her in about a week and that's starting to feel weird.

I take the stairs two at a time and join Zack downstairs. We walk out of the Football House together and start toward the field for practice.

"Dude, look at that fresh meat!" Zack says a little too loudly as we reach the quad. I have a pounding headache from all the drinks the douchebag dared me to have last night when we got home. I don't know how he can drink so much then wake up in the morning and be all jolly and shit like he didn't get hammered the night before. In his defense, I could've turned down the dare.

He punches me in the shoulder. "Are you seeing what I'm seeing?" he asks again. I look around, seeing all the different girls walking around the quad. Yes, they're pretty but that's not new so, I'm not sure what he's babbling about.

"Dude, that redheaded chick is hot!" Zack says, pointing in a different direction and my eyes follow. I can't help but nod in agreement when I realize he's talking about Zoe. I watch as she walks next to another girl I assume is her roommate. She looks so happy and carefree—like she belongs here, but she also stands out. Her red hair a striking contrast to the other girls.

I clear my throat and look back at Zack. I see the way his gaze lingers on her and I'm automatically on guard.

"What about the blonde one?" I ask, trying to distract him.

"The one with the glasses?" he asks in disbelief.

"Yeah, that one."

"Reminds me too much of Natasha—Natalia—whatever the hell her name was!" I assume he means one of the girls he's slept with.

"Oh, you mean one of your generic hookups?"

"Not generic. More like necessary maintenance."

I burst out laughing at my teammate's choice of words. "I don't want to know," I say, hoping to never have to hear one of his stories again.

"You already do. What can I say? The girls love it, and I have it. So, I use it."

"You should be careful," I warn him.

"I wear protection every time," he says with a wink and I shake my head. Zack will do what Zack wants to do and there's nothing we can do to stop it.

"What are you guys talking about?" Nick says startling us. "Fuck, Nick! Stop ambushing us like that," Zack says.

Nick grins. "I can't help that I have mad ninja skills."

We continue to walk slowly towards the field.

“We were talking about Zack’s hookups,” I say, hoping this new conversation pushes away the old one.

“The hot redhead over there,” Zack answers and I wish he hadn’t brought up Zoe because Nick stops to watch her too.

“Don’t tell me you already hooked up with her?” Nick asks Zack.

“Not yet,” Zack says with a shit-eating grin.

“Cut the shit, Hayes,” I practically growl.

Zack ignores me and says to Nick, “I haven’t seen those two around before.”

“The semester just started,” I say.

“Hey ladies,” Nick shouts, causing the people sitting on the quad to turn and stare. The Hunter Effect is what we’ve come to call this. It doesn’t matter which Hunter is in the area, they somehow have the power to command everyone’s attention. Baby brother loves it. Older brother hates it. And well, the sister is somewhere in the middle.

“Not interested,” Zoe shouts back without missing a step. I stare at her until she looks at me, a knowing smile playing on her lips. My breath hitches. I smile at her discreetly and wave from my place behind the guys.

“See you around,” Nick adds and I can tell he’s embarrassed that he wasn’t given the time of day. I laugh out loud.

That’s my girl.

Uh. Shit.

Friend—that’s my *friend*.

“What are you laughing at, Falcon?” Nick asks, turning to me with a sour look on his face.

I smile wider. “Just at seeing you fail, Little Hunter,” I tell him, ruffling his hair. When I see the look of determination in his eyes, I realize he’s taken my words as a challenge. I curse under my breath.

“Not failing. She’ll warm up to me. The semester’s just starting,” he says confidently.

Hell no, she won’t.

I’m about to tell him to back off when Zack says, “What are we doing tonight?”

Nick starts talking about a party he wants to go to and I take that moment to send Zoe a quick text.

Me: Sorry about my teammates. Remember that long line of guys waiting for you? I told you it would happen.

Zoe: Those are your friends?

I SMILE DOWN AT MY PHONE.

Me: Yup. I'll introduce you to them at some point, just not yet.

Zoe: Gotta wait to make sure I'll stick around?

Me: You're not going anywhere.

I JUST WANT IT TO BE US FOR NOW. AS SOON AS THE GUYS FIND OUT, they'll either hit on her, or assume her and I have something going on. I'm not ready to field questions. Zoe and I are just friends, but I have a feeling the guys won't take my word for it.

I hear Nick say, "Let's throw a party at the house!" just as I put my phone in my back pocket.

"We had one last night," I say, trying to be the voice of reason.

"That was just us drinking. That wasn't a party," Zack states matter-of-factly.

I turn to Nick. "Do you think Big Brother will let you?"

"Big Brother is too cuffed to Mia to pay any attention. When was the last time he spent the weekend at the house anyway?" Nick says, sounding a little bitter.

"He was there yesterday," I remind him.

"True, but I'm sure we can convince him." Nick rubs his hands together like he's coming up with a master plan. "We'll just convince Kaitlyn to convince Mia to convince Colton."

"That's a lot of work," Zack says, and I chuckle.

Nick shrugs. "You gotta do what you gotta do."

"Speaking of having to do something, do you think Coach is going to make us run a shit ton again today?"

We all groan. Summer training has been brutal and with kickoff starting soon, the practices are getting worse.

"You know he will," Nick says.

Let the semester begin.

16

ZOE

The next day, I familiarize myself with the campus again, and by the time I return to my room, I'm exhausted. Stretching myself out on my bed, I try to get some rest.

"Hey," Emma says, and I crack my eyes open a little to see her coming out of our bathroom with one towel wrapped around her head and the other around her body.

I point at the door. "Aren't you glad we have a bathroom inside of our dorm room and not out there?"

"Yes! I'm so freaking relieved. My last dorm had co-ed bathrooms outside. I had to carry all my clothes with me and you know, wait until really late to shower so I didn't run into anyone else

I laugh. "The horror!"

"Seriously. You do *not* want to be walking around a co-ed hall in just a towel."

"You're right. I don't." Seriously. That's too much exposure— way more than I'm comfortable with.

"Anyway," Emma says standing in front of her dresser.

"Yes?"

"I walked by your desk before and a few papers fell... I picked them up from the floor..." she says, opening both doors on her closet and staring inside. "I saw one from the hospital. It was your discharge papers. I didn't mean to..." She turns to look at me with guilty eyes.

Shit. I didn't put them away. I was looking at the instructions at mom's insistence.

"Um..." My mind races, trying to cover the truth with a believable lie.

"Are you... Err, do you..." Emma's unable to form a coherent sentence, and I know exactly what she wants to ask.

I sit up, resting my back against the headboard.

Her face flushes. "So, you don't have cancer anymore."

I shake my head. She walks towards me, crossing the invisible line between her side of the room and mine, and takes a seat on the edge of my bed. Slowly, tentatively, she extends her hand toward me.

"Is that why you took a year off ?" she asks, her voice low as if speaking to a wounded animal.

I clear my throat. "Yeah." "Are you okay?"

"Yes, I am."

"I'm sorry." She says those words that everyone automatically says when they find out.

I remove my hand from her hold. "Please don't be. Cancer sucks, but it happens. I'm not the first person to have it." And sadly, I won't be the last either.

"No, you're not, but that doesn't make it any less serious." She gets up, retreating to her bed. "What kind do—did you have?" she asks, no longer beating around the bush. That's another quality I've come to admire in the last week.

"ALL."

"Acute Lymphoblastic Leukemia. How long has it been? I know the five-year survival rate for children is eighty-five percent and for adults it's sixty-nine." She spews the statistics like it's her major and she's been studying it forever.

"Wow, you've done your research."

She shrugs. "I like researching. Also, sorry if that was insensitive. I just... When did you find out?"

I love that she goes from feeling bad for me, to throwing stats my way, to being concerned again.

"I got diagnosed a year ago. I did the whole stay in the hospital, the chemotherapy..."

"Did you get a bone marrow transplant?"

I'm once again taken aback by how much she knows. "No," I reply. "It hasn't been necessary."

She nods, pushing her glasses up the bridge of her nose. "You're in remission now then?"

"Yep. If I relapse, then I'd need a bone marrow transplant."

"It won't come to that," Emma says with absolute certainty.

"I know a little girl in the hospital who is currently going through the process," I say. "Her name's Maria. She's four years old."

"Man, fuck cancer," Emma says, jumping up from the bed.

"Woah, did you just swear?" I ask

She shrugs. "Sometimes I do. It just depends on how angry I am."

"I never thought I'd hear that word come out of your mouth."

She shrugs again. "Cancer deserves it."

I move to swing my legs over the side of the bed. "Thanks for caring, by the way."

She sits back down. "Don't mention it. Why didn't you tell me?"

"I wanted to start fresh. I didn't want anyone to pity me."

"I wasn't... I don't... I didn't mean to—"

I give her a knowing look and she closes her mouth. "I'm sorry."

"People don't intend to pity me, but it's a gut reaction. I'm beating cancer. There's no need to be sorry for me. I'm alive."

"I'm glad! You're a pretty darn good roommate and it would have taken a while to find a replacement," she says with a smile, and I feel the remaining tension dissipate.

"Wow, back to not swearing, huh?"

She grins. "I've met my swearing quota for the week. Stay tuned for next time."

"I'm anxiously waiting for it," I reply and then add "So, are you putting clothes on any time soon, or are we implementing a no-clothing zone?" I tease, knowing exactly how she'll react.

As expected, her cheeks redden immediately. "This is a clothing zone at all times! I'll put on mine."

She gets up from my bed and makes her way to her closet once again. "Hey, Zo," she says, turning to face me once again. "I know we haven't known each other for more than a week, but if you ever need to talk, I'm only like, two feet away."

"Thanks, I'll keep that in mind."

"So now that we've had the heavy emotion conversation, I've been meaning to ask you about that guy."

I pretend to have no idea what she's talking about. "Which guy?" I ask.

She throws a pair of pants onto her bed before continuing to rummage through her closet. "The handsome one from the quad."

"The one that called out to us? I don't know him," I reply.

"No, not that clown. I'm talking about the one behind him. The one that waved and smiled at you. The one, who I'm pretty sure, was texting you immediately after, if you smiling down at your phone was any indication."

I can't believe she noticed all that! I still act clueless though.

She gives me a knowing look. "The dark-haired guy next to the redhead and blonde? I saw how he was looking at you."

I shift uncomfortably. "You must've been seeing things."

She finally takes out a shirt and shuts the closet doors. "Things were very clear from where I was standing. I'm just saying."

"Could you just put some clothes on, lady?" I say, trying to distract her.

She grabs her pants. "Stop avoiding the topic. You know I'm not going to drop it!"

"I didn't know you were boy crazy," I tell her, finally giving in.

She walks into the bathroom to change, calling out, "Not at all, but you should know I am crazy about romance books."

"Noted!"

"What are we doing today, anyway?" she asks.

"What we do every day, Pinky; try to take over the world!" I respond, following it up with my rehearsed devilish laughter.

"You're such a weirdo!"

"I think I'm pretty normal." I lay on my stomach. I'm still exhausted but I know I won't be falling asleep any time soon. "When you finally put clothes on, do you want to go for some coffee?"

"Sure, but just so you know, I hate coffee. Hot chocolate is my drink of choice," she says, coming back into the room fully clothed.

"Who are you?" I reply, getting off the bed. "How can you not like coffee? How do you even function?"

"I'm Emma, your roommate, friend and avid reader," she says, extending her hand to me.

I wave it off. "And you say you aren't weird? Fine, let's go to the café and get a coffee and a hot chocolate."

"Okay! Let me fix my hair. I'll be ready in a jiffy," Emma says, running into the bathroom once again.

Again with that word. *Who says* jiffy?

17

JESSE

Before going to practice, some of the guys and I decide to stop and grab a bite to eat. I haven't seen Zoe since that one time on the quad a week ago, and it's not because I haven't wanted to. It's just that Coach is running us all into the ground in preparation for the upcoming season.

I'm the last one through the doors of the cafeteria, and I glance around, spotting Zoe sitting at one of the tables with her roommate. None of the guys have noticed her yet, so I don't draw any attention to her either. I trail behind them, ordering my food last. When I'm sure my teammates have gone to our usual table, I suck in a breath and walk towards her....

Zoe smiles as I reach the table. God, I've missed that smile. "Hey."

"Hi," she responds.

I turn to look at her roommate, who's reading on an e-reader. "You must be Emma," I say.

She looks from me to Zoe, a knowing smile on her lips before saying, "That's right. And you're the guy from the quad."

"Jesse," I supply, but she's already looking back down at her book.

"Have a seat," Zoe says.

I sit down beside her, our shoulders brushing in the process. "How's everything going so far?" I ask.

She shrugs. "Not bad. It's different than I remember." "Yeah, a lot of things have changed."

"That they have," she says, her tone reminiscent.

I look to Emma, waiting to see if she's going to join the conversation.

"Don't mind her. She's always getting lost in one of her romance books," Zoe says, shaking her head.

I nod. "Got it... Hey, so, I'm sorry I haven't been around much." The truth is, I really miss seeing her every day.

Zoe waves her hands in the air, dismissing my statement. "Don't worry about it. I've had a long line of guys to entertain me."

I know she's only teasing me, but I still can't help but feel my jealousy surge. I tamp it back down before saying, "You're still going to make some room for me in that busy calendar, right?"

"When you make some room in yours for me." She picks up an apple and takes a bite. With that one simple action, I'm taken back to the time we spent in the hospital. In the cafeteria. I'm shocked to realize that the memories of being there aren't at all what they used to be. They don't fill me with a feeling of hopelessness or pain. Rather, they remind me of meeting her.

"I'm sorry. Football practices and team bonding shit has been all consuming," I tell her.

She shrugs. "I get it."

"It still sucks."

"Does it get better?"

I nod. "Oddly enough, yes. I'll still have practice, but not as often with all the games. You're still coming to my games, right?" I ask, and Emma clears her throat noisily, her eyes still scanning the digital page.

Zoe frowns at her roommate before saying, "I'll think about it."

She's baiting me, but I miss this banter—more than I thought I would.

"Hey, Falcon, wanna introduce us?" Zack calls and I turn to my left, looking directly at him across the room.

I curse under my breath. "Not really," I whisper loud enough for Zoe to hear. Her expression falls and I kick myself for saying it out loud. "Sorry, I... I don't want them to... he..." I stumble over my words trying to justify to her why I don't want them to meet her. I guess it's hard to explain something to someone else when you don't quite understand it yourself.

"Don't worry about it," she says waving me off, but I can see the hurt in her eyes.

Bringing my hand to the back of my head, I try to think of a way to dig myself out of the hole I've made. "It's not you. They're sort of... a lot." That's the best I can come up with.

"Yeah, Falcon, who are your new friends?" Nick shouts.

I shoot daggers at the guys before turning my attention back to Zoe. "I... I'll just go... we have practice in a few and I still need to eat." I don't want Nick or Zack coming over here and taking it upon themselves to find out more about her—or worse.

"Is it okay if I text you later, Red?" I ask, feeling like a giant ass.

She looks at me with her beautiful hazel eyes and smiles. "Sure." Her smile gives me the assurance I need to know I'm not screwing it all up. I get up and head over to the counter, picking up my sandwich and drink, and walking back to the guys, who are watching me with amusement.

"So, *that's* the girl you've been keeping from us, Falcon?" Chase asks. I stare at him, a little stunned. Generally speaking, he's the least interested in girls.

Chase, Zack, and Nick look over their shoulders in the direction of Emma and Zoe, then look back at me.

"Wait, are these the same girls from the quad?" Zack asks as I take a seat next to him. He's fixated on the pair, and I hit him on the shoulder to stop him from staring.

"Damn, Falcon. You work fast," Nick adds. I shake my head, but don't say anything. I don't want to explain anything—not yet.

"So, you're saying you knew who they were and didn't say anything?" Nick accuses.

I smile, but it doesn't quite reach my eyes. "Yes."

Zack looks at me and shakes his head. "That's cold, man."

"No wonder they were immune to my charms. You probably told them to ignore me," Nick says, like that's the only reason a girl wouldn't fall at his feet.

I shake my head and take a bite of my sandwich. "I didn't say anything to them. I didn't need to. You *do* know your *charms*—" I say the last word with air quotes, "—don't work on everyone, right?" Some girls just aren't into what he's selling. Not many girls, but some, and I'm sure Zoe is one of them.

"Are you going to sit with them again?" Zack asks.

"Nope, I talked to them for a while." Mostly to Zoe, and definitely not for long enough.

"Why don't we all join them?" Zack, the grinning idiot, asks.

"They're busy." My words are clipped, but I can't help it.

"Too busy for us, but not too busy for you?" Nick asks in disbelief. The asshole knows I don't want him near them—near her.

"If they're okay with you joining them, I'm sure it'd be fine if we did too. Which one are you going for? I'd love to get my hands on that pretty redhead," Zack adds, and I'm on my feet in an instant. My pulse is pounding in my ears, and I take a moment to register the look of shock on everyone's faces. Clearing my throat, I take my seat before I do something stupid.

Zack lifts his hands in defeat. "The redhead is yours, got it!"

"I'm still down to get with the other one—for a night," Nick says, unable to help himself.

I hiss through gritted teeth, "Leave Zoe and Emma alone."

"Zoe and Emma. I like those names. I bet the redhead is Emma," Zack says again, deliberately testing my patience.

"No, Zoe is the redhead. I won't warn you guys again about staying away from them."

"We'll let your girl be. The other one though, I may call dibs," Nick says again, and I give him the coldest stare.

"She's not even your type."

"Do I have a type?" Nick shoots back with a devil-may-care smile.

I sit there wondering why I'm here instead of with Zoe. Man, if I didn't love these guys, things would be a lot different.

"I don't think you do," Chase chimes in and we all burst out laughing.

Nick shrugs, not at all bothered. "What can I say? I give all girls an equal chance to please me."

"Please stop talking," I tell him, hoping the girls don't notice we're talking about them.

"When was the last time you got any? Is talking about my active sex life making you feel deprived?"

"Don't start," I say in a low voice.

Noting the change in the atmosphere, Zack steps in and says, "Anyway, are you guys ready for the crazy parties we'll be having this year?"

"Hell yeah!" Nick shouts, causing people to stop their conversations and tune into ours. Chase doesn't say anything, and neither do I. The party planning stays in the competent hands of Nick and Zack since they're the ones that thought it out last year—after every game, we party.

"We have the welcome party this weekend. Remember we need to sort everything out," I remind them. From the corner of my eye, I spot Zoe and Emma walking towards the trashcans near our table. My eyes are trained on them as they laugh at something Zoe says and I wish I was part of the conversation too.

As they pass, Zoe gives me a small reserved smile. In response, I give her what I hope is a sly wink. I don't know why, it just felt like the right thing to do and I spend a second analyzing it. She and Emma discard their empty containers and head towards the exit.

"So yes, we have everything we need for the party," Zack adds in a very 'end of business' fashion, which reminds me I've tuned out for a part of the conversation. It's insane how well put together they are when it comes to parties—I wish they did everything else with as much dedication.

The door to the café opens and I turn in my seat, hoping to see Zoe once again. I'm disappointed when two guys walk in instead. From the corner of my eye, I see Nick's shoulders stiffen, his back ramrod straight. On top of the table, his hands ball into fists.

He attempts to get up, but Chase is there, pushing him back down by the shoulders. "Easy," Chase says.

The guys walk by our table, and one of them mutters something under his breath to the other. All I hear from my seat is Kaitlyn's name. In the blink of an eye, Chase leaps from his seat, grabs him by the neck and shoves his face into the café table.

I stand up. "Fuck!" I try to pry Chase from the guy before he does some real damage, but Chase shoves me away. "Zack!" I shout calling in back up when I notice Nick's nostrils flare. I head over to him and hold him back knowing he's seconds away from joining the fight.

"On it," Zack replies, locking Chase's arms down and pinning them to his sides. Zack does his best to haul Chase away, putting himself between him and the guy who had seemingly pissed off the defensive lineman.

The guy who Chase attacked stands up, his eyes wide and his chest heaving. His friend grabs him by the arm and leads him out of the café.

I have no idea what's just happened. By the look on Zack's face, he hasn't got a clue either. I know neither Chase or Nick are about to explain it to us so I clear my throat. "We should get to practice."

ZOE

The moment we step outside the café, Emma exclaims excitedly, "I saw that! He just winked at you!"

"What are you talking about? He was just blinking." I choose to downplay it—mostly because I think I should. After all, he doesn't even want me to meet his friends.

Emma gives me an incredulous look. "With one eye? Blinking with one eye? Really? That's reserved for one-eyed individuals and pirates!"

I laugh. "He may have had something in his eye."

"Yeah, YOU!" She throws her hands into the air, outraged at my apparent lack of understanding.

"Anyway..." I try to change the topic, but fail when I blank on what to follow up with.

She takes a deep breath, preparing to explain things to me. "No, no, not 'anyway'. You won't get out of it that easily. He walked into the café, spotted you and then joined our table."

"He spotted us," I correct.

"He doesn't know me. He's seen me once," she deadpans. "But you made it seem like you didn't quite know him when I asked you. The way you two were talking just now makes it seem like you guys have known each other forever."

"He and I may have met over the summer," I say, smiling as we start walking back to the dorm.

"When in the summer? Weren't you in hospital and then confined to your home this summer? Was he in the hospital with you? Oh, my God, does he have cancer? Did he have cancer? Is he—"

I interrupt Emma before she confuses herself. "If you stopped throwing out a million questions a second, I could try answering them."

She sighs. "Fine, go ahead!"

I laugh. "Thank you. He was an intern at the hospital."

Her eyes light up."Oh! I read a book like this. The guy is an intern, who meets the girl at a hospital and was immediately attracted to her. Then they get together and steamy stuff happens." Emma's face goes red when she sees the look in my eye. She knows she's just unintentionally confirmed to me that her reading list isn't so squeaky clean.

"Steamy stuff, huh?" She blushes. "Emma, first, what kind of stories are you reading? Second, this is not that kind of story," I say.

"But it could be! He seems interested," she continues, purposefully avoiding my question. I don't know how interested he seems when the moment his friends are around, he wants the earth to swallow him whole.

We close the distance to our dorm, and I try and explain to her that there's nothing between Jesse and me. "We kind of became friends this summer since he was at the hospital a lot for an internship. And I was there for treatment."

"And then you saw him every day and realized you were meant to be!" Emma cuts in excitedly.

I have to stop myself from rolling my eyes. "Not a book. Not a fairytale. We're just friends." I say friends hesitantly because aside from exchanging messages, and seeing him at the café a few minutes ago, I haven't spent as much time with him as I used to— as much time as we spent together last summer.

"A friendship is a start; it could turn into more. He did wink at you!" For someone so interested in science, math, and facts, my roommate is a bit of a romantic, which I guess I already knew based on all the romance books she's read in the last week.

"Keep your fairytales in books, woman! We live in the real world," I tell her. Someone throws a Frisbee and it lands near our feet. I grab it and toss it back.

"Thank you," the group of students yell back and I nod in response.

"Do you believe in all that football-player-falls-in-love-with- nerd stuff from books?" I ask her. Part of me is trying to make the point that those things don't happen in real life, but a smaller part of me hopes she does believe in it—because that's what my story with Jesse, if there ever was one, would be.

"To be honest, it's easier to believe it in books. I don't know if I'd buy it in real life," she says, and I think my expression changes because she adds, "but you never know. It could happen."

We walk the rest of the way to the dorm, talking about classes and life. It's insane that this has become my new normal—just having a conversation with my roommate about a guy, school, and life. I never thought I'd ever have the ability to think about my future again. But I can.

18

JESSE

The weekend comes around faster than I expected, and yet at the same time, it feels like it takes forever. It's probably because I haven't seen Zoe again. I still haven't gotten to hang out with her. All we have is messages going back and forth, and while that's nice, I need more. Leaving my room and shutting the door behind me, I take the steps downstairs two at a time to join the guys in the living room.

"Who's ready to party?" Zack shouts from the top of the stairs. Some of the freshmen moving the couch down to the basement in preparation for our annual welcome party glance up at him and grin.

Nick comes out of the kitchen, beer in hand. "I'm ready!" he shouts back.

"Can either of you help me move this chair?" I ask, upset about being roped into helping in the first place. Each year I say I won't do it, and each year I end up here. Sometimes I think I'm too nice.

Nick puts his beer down on the nearest counter and finally walks over to me. "Where's Colton?" he asks.

Coming down the stairs, Zack replies, "Where do you think?"

"He's fucking whipped." Nick says the word *whipped* like it's the worst thing that could happen to a guy.

Feeling the need to step in, I add, "He's happy." I immediately regret it.

"Oh yeah, happy. He's *happy*," Nick mocks and Zack and a few others join him. They think being in a relationship is some sort of burden. The sad thing is, none of them know any better.

"Cut the shit and get this stuff downstairs already," Chase says from behind us.

Nick salutes him before picking up his end of the couch and helping me move it downstairs.

"Smartass," Chase mutters, cracking a bit of a smile. Chase Boulder. He's as intimidating as Colton, but unlike Colton, he hasn't had a girl soften him up. He may be a hard-ass—a little rough around the edges—but he cares about all of us.

"Do you think Colton is coming tonight?" Nick asks as we descend the stairs.

Coming in right behind us carrying a lamp, Zack says, "He kind of has to—he is the president and all!"

We reach the basement and set the couch on the floor. "He'll probably show his face for like a minute and then leave. He may be president, but he does what he wants," one of the red shirts on the team, Alex, says as he and another freshman reorganize the furniture. Nick, Zack and I turn to him immediately, the same thought running through all of our minds.

Nick stalks over to the kid. "What did you say?" he asks, enunciating each word.

"I j-j-just... I—" Alex stammers. He looks over at his friend, who has taken a step back.

"You *what?*" Zack adds, standing by Nick's side now. I can see the fear in the freshman's eyes, and I sit back, doing my best to hold back my laughter.

Alex's eyes volley between Zack and Nick. "You...you guys talk about him being absent all the time. I was just..."

"We earned that right by not only being his teammates, but his family," Nick replies.

"You haven't earned shit," Zack adds.

Alex looks down at the floor and then back up at the guys. "I'm sorry," he says.

"Alright, that's enough," I tell them, and Zack and Nick burst out laughing.

"Did you see how scared he was?" Zack says, pointing at the poor freshman.

The other freshman, who's name I should probably learn, smiles. "You...you guys were only joking?"

"Sort of. We know you don't know any better—just don't do it again," Nick says, turning around and heading up the stairs. Zack and I follow behind him as the two freshmen stay behind and resume their jobs.

"Tonight, I'm drinking until I can't see color," Zack announces the moment we reach the living room.

I look at him with concern. "Do you really think that's a good idea?" I ask, knowing he's going to ignore me anyway. Zack kind of plays by his own rules.

"Isn't that the point of these parties?" he says, heading over to the kitchen to get himself a beer. I don't respond because he's right—there really is no other point to these parties. If I weren't on the team, and if these guys weren't my brothers, I wouldn't bother attending.

Nick walks by me with another lamp in his hand. "Do you think your friends will show up?" I know he's talking about Zoe and Emma, and I almost tell him to back off, but realize that may not be the right approach. Nick likes challenges, and if he feels like that's what this is, it'll only make him more determined.

"Who knows? They're juniors," I reply. I don't know if Zoe is up for it, and from what I know about Emma, she's majoring in something science-related and loves books—parties and football games are not her thing.

Nick looks like he's mulling this information over before he replies. "We both know that not just freshmen show up to our parties."

"Yeah, but if they don't regularly attend other parties, why would they come to one of ours?"

"That's nonsense," he retorts. "Everyone wants to come to our parties."

"You do know that if everyone in the entire school came to our parties, we would need a bigger house?"

He rolls his eyes. "Just keep an eye out and let me know if your *friend* with the red hair shows up."

I nod, knowing if she were to show up, I wouldn't be the one to tell him. Not a chance in the world.

ZOE

Jesse: Hey, are you coming to the welcome party? – Good Doctor.

Me: What party?

I STRETCH OUT ON MY BED, FEELING THE WEIGHT OF MY LETHARGY LIKE A blanket. Classes haven't started yet, but I've had to meet with a few different administration people to ensure that—as they put it— 'my transition back into Bragan is smooth.'

"Do you know of a party happening tonight?" I ask Emma.

She looks at me from over the top of her paperback. "Me? No. I have no idea."

"Huh…" I lick my lips. "Another romance novel?"

She shrugs, marking her page and closing the book. "You sound surprised."

"That's the third one this week."

Her eyes crinkle in the corners as she laughs. "I'm not even close to breaking my weekly record."

I look down at my phone—still no reply. "You've been here for three years now..."

Setting her paperback down, she shrugs and says, "And I've never gone to a party. Why do you ask?"

I try to look disinterested. "Oh, just Jesse asked if we were going."

"Oh, Jesse," she says in an 'I told you so' kind of way. "Why didn't you just say you knew him when we saw him and his friends on the quad?

"I told him I didn't want any unnecessary attention. He's a football player. I don't want to ride his coat tails."

She nods. "You don't seem like the coat-tail-riding type."

"Psht, I love the attention," I respond sarcastically.

"We're going to get along just fine."

I raise my brows at her. "I thought you'd already figured this out!"

"Eh, I was still testing my theory."

My phone beeps with an incoming message. "I'm like your best friend already," I tell her as I open the notification.

Jesse: The Welcome Party we host every year for freshmen. – Good Doctor

Me: I was here freshmen year and don't recall this party. Also, stop calling yourself that.

I glance over at Emma who's already picked up her book again.

"Does the Welcome Party for Freshmen ring a bell?" She shakes her head without giving me a second look.

"Fine, I'll let you read your smut."

Without looking up, she throws a pillow at me.

She didn't deny it though.

Jesse: The first two years were lame. It's much better now. Are you coming? Maybe you can bring your roommate? It's tonight... Also, is Good Intern better?

Me: Tonight?! I'm gonna pass... You're not an intern anymore.

Jesse: Come on! You know you want to hang out with me. I miss hanging out with you.

I can't hold back my smile. Spending time with Jesse sounds heavenly, but I don't know that a party is where I want to do that.

Me: Eh, not really. I think I'll opt for a quiet night in with Emma.

Jesse: You're killing me, Evans. Bring Emma and come have some fun, even if it's only for an hour. It'll make my night.

I bite my lip to keep from smiling. I don't want Emma to see the way he makes me react, the way just his messages can put a smile on my face.

Me: I'll think about it.

Jesse: Remember you promised you'd make time for me.

Me: STOP trying to guilt me into going to your party.

Jesse: I won't stop if it's working... Is it?

I smile.

Me: Maybe.

Jesse: You know you have nothing else to do tonight. You're probably already in your dorm, wearing pajamas and lying in bed.

I look down at myself to see that he's right on the money with his prediction.

Me: You may be right. If I can convince Emma to come with me, I'll go.

Jesse: I'll send you the address. Tell Emma I'll buy her ice cream.

Me: You may need more than ice cream to convince Emma to drop her book and go to a party.

I look at my roommate who is frantically flipping back and forth between two pages, her mouth open in shock.

Jesse: I'll give her anything she wants.

Me: I'll let you know if she accepts that offer. Oh... and Jesse?

I tell him and wait anxiously for him to respond.

Jesse: Yeah?

Me: I miss you too.

I type out the words and send the message as quickly as I can before I lose the courage. The small icon at the bottom of the screen shows me he's typing, but then it stops. It does that a few more times before it stops again. I set my phone down and turn to my roommate once again, this time looking for a distraction to calm my rapidly beating heart.

"Hey Emma?" I use my sweet voice to pry my roommate away from her book once more.

She looks at me. "Yes..." she answers knowingly, drawing out the word.

I clear my throat. "Do you *want* to go to the Welcome Party tonight?"

"No," she says without any hesitation.

"Would anything change your mind?"

Returning her attention to her book, she says, "Nope."

Well, I tried. I got shut down, and I'm staying in. Maybe next time! Getting up, I head over to my desk and pull out my journal. I started journaling when I was first diagnosed with ALL; I wanted to leave something behind, a legacy of some sort. But since I hadn't done much with my life yet, I figured I could at least leave some words for others to find.

Now, I keep writing because you never know when life can end. I write my thoughts, my goals, and my regrets and if I'm lucky enough to live and see my future children grow up, then maybe I pass this on to them so that they can have a glimpse of my journey. So that they, too, can appreciate each and every day of their lives.

I LOSE MYSELF IN THE SOUND OF THE PEN MOVING OVER THE PAPER, THE rustle of the turning pages, only realizing I've been writing for almost two hours when my phone pings. I look around the room to find Emma asleep, her book resting on her face.

Carefully, I take the novel and place it on the shelf above her desk. I pick up my phone to find a text from Jesse. I smile instinctively. I haven't even read the words, but that's the way I react at the mere thought of him. I'm old enough to know that I definitely have a crush on him and it's completely his fault. He's too sweet, kind, and caring. He's unbelievably handsome. And, well, clearly out of my league so I'll settle for having him as a friend.

Jesse: You coming, Evans?

Me: No, sir. Staying in tonight. Have fun though!

Jesse: You're breaking my heart, Red. I'd have more fun if you were here :(

Me: I'm sure you'll survive, Falcon.

Jesse: I may not; you never know.

I may not have gone to the party, but from the speed his replies are coming in, maybe I'm not missing out on much—well aside from missing out on the opportunity to see him.

Getting comfortable in bed, we text back and forth until I eventually fall asleep.

19

ZOE

For the first time in a long time, I take the stairs rather than the elevator out of my dorm. I'm blaming it on nerves; I feel like I have a whole swarm of butterflies in the pit of my stomach, all of them flapping around wildly in an effort to get out. I know I have that feeling for one reason, and one reason only: Jesse.

"Man, why does it feel like I haven't seen you in ages?" he says as soon as I open the lobby door.

I try to hide my smile. "Because you haven't. You abandoned me weeks ago." I take a step closer, letting the door shut behind me I take him in—the length of his hair, the exact shade of blue of his eyes. I don't know how I'm supposed to greet him—it's been so long since we've been alone together.

"Come here," he says, making the decision for me. He envelopes me in a bear hug, one that reminds me that I miss him so damn much even though I shouldn't. I hug him back, feeling the strength of his arms and smelling his cologne. Why does he always smell so good?

"Reacquainting yourself with the way I smell?"

I pull back right away, feeling my cheeks reddening. "No!"

He grins. "It's okay. You haven't sniffed me in a while. I get that you have to become familiar with me again."

My eyes widen. "Are you comparing me to a dog?"

"Absolutely not. I was recalling your birthday and how you took your time breathing me in."

"Can we just forget that ever happened?" I beg.

"No, ma'am. I'm going to remember that for the rest of our lives."

I don't know why the fact that he says 'ours' makes me smile, but it does.

I roll my eyes to faint annoyance. "Whatever. So, what are we doing today?" I ask. When he messaged me and we finally decided on a time to hang out, he told me all I needed to do was wear comfortable clothes and wait for him at the lobby of my dorm at 5pm.

"It's a surprise," he replies. He runs his hands through his hair and adds, "Are you ready to go?"

I nod.

"So, how's the first, what week, week and a half now, going?" he asks as we walk shoulder-to-shoulder.

I shrug. "Kind of tiring, to be honest. I don't love my classes, and I'm probably the oldest student in all of them." I wanted to come back to school, to study, but taking classes has reminded me of how much I hated it.

"First of all, no one likes classes. Well, maybe Emma," he jokes. "Second," he says, counting with his fingers, "It's not your fault you had to miss a year. Plus, I think students are taking longer to graduate high school so you're probably just about the same age as they are."

We keep walking until we reach the student lot. "Are we going off campus?"

"Not really, but it's better if we drive there," he says. Jesse leads me to his car, and I'm about to open the passenger door when he stops me.

"Here, let me," he says, opening the door. Smiling widely, I get inside, putting on my seatbelt as I watch him walk around and get in.

"So, we're not going off campus, but we're driving there? Could I have some clues as to what we're doing?"

He shakes his head at me. "You're just going to have to wait."

"Next time, I'll just have to say *no* when you ask to hang out," I tease.

He grips his chest. "You wouldn't dare."

"So, tell me what we're doing!" I whine.

"Good things come to those who wait," he says, pulling out of the parking spot. I roll my eyes and turn on the radio.

By the time the second random pop song is coming to an end, the car slows to a stop. I look out the windshield to find us parking in one of the football field designated parking lots.

"Are you kidding me?"

"Nope," he says with a chuckle as he shuts off the car and gets out. I follow him.

"We are NOT watching a football game right now!"

He gives me a long look. "Not this time, but maybe the next."

Why are we here if we aren't watching a football game?

He opens the backdoor of his car, grabbing a backpack. "Are you ready?"

My eyes narrow. "I don't know. How can I tell you I'm ready if I don't know what we're doing?"

He shuts the car door and locks it. "Let's go," he says, finding my hand. It feels so foreign, yet so familiar—like a missing part of me I haven't felt in a long time. He pulls me closer to the football field, but I don't try to catch up because I'm afraid the moment I do, he'll let go.

"Is there something going on here?" I ask the moment we reach the side doors.

He uses his ID to get inside. "Just the two of us hanging out," he says casually.

I point at the facility. "Inside there?"

"Oh, Evans, it's killing you not knowing what's happening, isn't it?"

"Yes!"

He clicks his tongue at me. "I thought you were going to let lose;

enjoy life!"

"I'm pretty sure that doesn't include breaking into the stadium!"

He gives me an incredulous look. "Zoe, did my ID card open the door?"

I nod.

"Do you think if I were breaking in, I'd be able to do that with my student ID?"

He's got a point.

"But maybe I'm not supposed to be here!" I try and reason.

"You're supposed to be with me." Those words—his words... I'm supposed to be with him. And while I know he means here, right now, I can't help but think about more. I haven't forgotten the fact that he still hasn't let go of my hand.

He opens the door and we walk through. A few seconds later, I'm met by an enormous field, numbers drawn on the green grass. I look around to see all the empty benches, and right now, in this moment, this place feels so surreal.

I haven't seen a football game in person—only on TV—but I can envision the fans seated on the benches, cheering for their teams. To see this place empty just seems odd. Out of place. Kind of like me.

"Isn't it amazing?" he asks, looking at me with a contagious smile.

I take it all in. "It is," I find myself saying out loud.

Jesse starts walking towards the ten-yard line, pulling me behind him. He drops his bag. "Let's settle down here."

"Watcha got in there?" I ask, curious. He pulls out a football. "So, we're here for you to practice?"

He brings his arm around my shoulders. "No. I'm going to teach you how to play football. That way, when you finally come to the game, you'll know what's going on!"

"Who said I was going to come your football games?" I ask, knowing I'll be there cheering him on.

"You have no choice. It's a requirement of our friendship."

"Since when?"

"Since we're going to be friends forever."

"Forever?" I ask in a horrified voice.

"Don't act like you don't want to be stuck with me forever," he says jokingly. He has no idea how right he is. I wouldn't mind forever with him.

He pulls me toward the center of the field. "You better have brought some food with you too," I tell him.

"I did, but you only get it if you earn it."

"And how do I do that?"

He smiles. "Just stand here. I'll stand about ten yards away. I'll throw the football and you'll catch it. That's step one."

"Aren't you a kicker? I thought I was learning the rules of the game."

"To learn the rules, you have to play. I may be a kicker, but football is football." He says this like it explains everything. Nevertheless, I follow his instructions and stand in my place.

He throws the football at me a few times, and after the fifth attempt, I finally catch it.

"Yes!" Jesse exclaims, running over and lifting me in the air. I'm reminded of the first time he did that at the hospital when I told him I was cancer-free. That day, the gesture felt strange to the both of us, but as he spins me around, I can't help laughing and reveling in the feeling of his touch, the sound of his laughter.

When he lowers me to the ground, he skims his fingers down the length of my arms. The intensity of his stare causes me to shiver, but then he grins and the intensity of the moment is gone.

"Let's see if that time wasn't just a fluke."

Backing up to his original position, he throws the ball to me again. I wait for it to reach me, bring my hands out, and catch it against my chest once again. I'm definitely getting the hang of this. "Alright, you've earned your food!" Jesse says.

"Thank goodness!" I shout.

He takes the football from my hands and brings his arm around my shoulder. "Good work today, Evans."

"Thanks, Coach," I respond, playfully patting him on the back. We start walking towards his bag, and I enjoy the way his arm feels around my shoulders. "So, what'd you bring for lunch?" I ask.

"What do you think?" he says, looking at me with eyebrows raised.

I stop mid-step. "Turkey sandwiches?"

He nods enthusiastically. "And apples!"

"I can't believe that's what you brought," I tell him, sitting down on the turf.

"I had to reinvent our first date." When the words leave his mouth, my heart somersaults inside my chest. *Date.* Is that what this is? Because that it's what I want it to be.

He starts searching through his bag and pulls out two wrapped sandwiches, apples, and Gatorades. It's crazy how the uttering of one little word has thrown *me* off kilter, but he seems just fine. "Make sure you drink a lot. You've gotta restore electrolytes," he says handing the Gatorade over to me.

"Yes, sir."

"So, what do you think about football?" he asks, passing the sandwich and apple over to me.

"Not bad. That was actually fun," I tell him honestly.

"So, you'll be at my next game?" He takes a bite of his lunch. I take in his every action, unable to stop myself from admiring this handsome man seated in front of me.

"I'll think about it," I tease him once again. I know I'll definitely go to his game, but I love how it feels to have him ask me—to have him want me to cheer him on, watch him.

"You have to now, otherwise, you'll have to pay for this mini football camp we just had."

"I didn't ask for this! I shouldn't have to pay for it," I whine, unwrapping my own sandwich.

He nods. "True. But your life is so much better because of it. So, you should at least come see me play."

"We'll see."

"You play a hard game, Evans," he says, setting down the remainder of his sandwich and opening his drink.

"So do you, Falcon," I remind him. And while I do mean football, I also mean with my heart.

20

JESSE

Despite the chill wind and intermittent rain, I'm back at the place I used to spend most of my time off. To be honest, I feel guilty that I haven't been here in a month. That's the longest I've gone without taking this same road, following the same path.

"I'm sorry for not replacing these sooner," I tell Hayley, switching out the old lilies for fresh ones.

"The last few weeks have been crazy. Remember I told you all about how the internship was going the last time I was here?" I pause as if waiting for confirmation I know will never come. "I didn't tell you about someone I'd met." I hang my head, a little ashamed for keeping this from her.

"I told you about Maria, but I didn't mention that I met another girl. I should've told you about her earlier, but—" I run my fingers through my hair, feeling like invisible walls are closing in on me.

"I didn't want you to think I was replacing you." I'd never do that.

I start playing with the grass next to her headstone. I wait to see if I can feel something. Anything.

Turning, I look around the almost empty cemetery. There are only a couple of people around and each of their expressions mirror my own. An older man stands in front of a grave, staring longingly at it. I can see from the lost look in his face that he'd do whatever was possible to switch places with whomever rests there. Or maybe that's just me assuming he feels the same way I do. A few feet behind him, a middle-aged woman is looking at the sky. She's probably questioning why her loved one was taken away from her, why her time with them was cut short? I wonder the same thing.

"I'm sorry I haven't come to see you." I touch the cold stone. "I know if you were here, you'd say something like, 'Jess, I don't know why you keep coming to this empty grave. I'm not here anymore. I'm in heaven looking over you. Stop holding onto the past. Live!'" I smile, remembering the sound of her voice, the constant smile on her face. Even at the end of her life, she never ceased to amaze me.

"I know you aren't here, but it feels wrong to let this place be forgotten—to let *you* be forgotten. I don't want to stop remembering you, stop talking to you..."

"So, yeah, I met this girl..." I don't know why I keep avoiding this conversation, but I owe it to Hayley. I even owe it to Zoe. "Her name is Zoe, and she was a patient at the hospital. I didn't really think I'd be close to her, or anyone else for that matter, but it just happened. She has some qualities that remind me of you, but she's also very different.

"She's got short red hair. She told me it used to be long before the cancer came... how much she missed it..." I sigh and kick out my legs. "When she talked about losing it all, it reminded me of you. You told me how important hair was for girls. I never understood it. I thought you looked breathtakingly beautiful with it both short and long. Whatever way you had it, it looked amazing on you... The same is true for her." I shake my head, stopping myself from thinking about Zoe in the same way I think about Hayley.

"Anyway," I say, "I know I haven't been here in a while, but I'll get better at that."

I don't want to forget her.

I can't.

ZOE

I TAKE THE STEPS UP TO THE HOSPITAL ONE AT A TIME. IT'S BEEN A couple of weeks since I last came in for a checkup, just enough time that I *almost* forgot I was stuck here for months.

Thinking back on the last year of my life, it's kind of unbelievable how far I've come. I mean, I beat cancer, resumed college, and met Emma. I even have Jesse in my life.

Fiona greets me the moment I walk in through the doors of the oncology floor.

I run into her open arms, embracing her. I've missed seeing her so much. "Hi, Fi."

"Someone's in a good mood," she says, hugging me back.

"Life is good," I tell her and I mean it.

"Glad to hear it!"

"How's everything here?" I ask a little more cautiously.

"You know, same as always." I know what she means by that. I was here long enough to hear about the good days, where the kids overcame illness, and the bad days when the illness overcame the kids.

"How's Maria?" I ask, feeling guilty that I haven't been by in the last couple of weeks. Making the transition into a full-time student and adjusting to all that entails has taken up a lot of my time. That plus Emma and Jesse.

Still, that's no excuse for not visiting her—not a good one anyway.

"She's holding on. We're hoping the bone marrow transplant works."

"Can I go see her?" When I was a patient, I had free reign of the hospital, but now as an outpatient, I feel like I have to ask.

"Of course. You know the way. After you're done, head over to the treatment room. We just need to run some blood tests."

"Thanks, Fi." I walk over to Maria's room. With each step, I pray she'll be as lucky as I am. I can't even fathom the pain she must have gone through—the pain she's still going through. Well, that's a lie, I can imagine it.

I pop my head into the room "Knock, knock." Robert is sitting on the chair near the bed, while Martha sits on the side of the bed, playing peek-a-boo with her baby girl. Maria's laughter fills the room and my heart all at the same time.

"Look who came to visit!" Robert exclaims, using the sweet voice he reserves for his granddaughter.

"Zoe!" Maria shouts, clapping her hands.

I step into the room. "Hi, beautiful."

"Hey, Zo. It's so great to see you!" Martha gets up from the bed and meets me halfway, embracing me. She hugs me for a few beats before finally letting go.

"I've missed you guys so much. I've missed you especially," I tell Maria.

"I missed you too! When are you coming back?" she asks. To visit? More often. To stay? Hopefully never.

"I'll come visit soon. Sorry I haven't had a chance to stop by."

"It's okay. Can we play a game?" Maria asks, my transgressions long forgotten.

"Sure, we can! What do you want to play?" Martha takes a seat next to Robert and I take her spot on the bed like I have many times before. The only difference this time is that after it's over, I won't be heading to my own room down the hall.

"Can we play 'I spy'?" she asks.

I nod. "I spy, with my little eye, a very pretty little girl."

"Is it me?" she responds, excited to have guessed.

"You're still so good at this game!" I tell her and she smiles proudly. It's these little things—small things like playing this game that makes long days feel a little shorter, go by a little quicker. I play with Maria and catch up with Robert and Martha for a couple of minutes until it's time for my check-up. After it's done and the doctor clears me once again, I return to Maria's room and try and make her smile a few more times.

"THANK YOU," MARTHA TELLS ME AS SHE WALKS ME OUT THE DOOR TWO hours later.

"I'm sorry I haven't been by."

"Don't be. Seeing you out there instead of in here gives me hope that one day I'll see my little girl doing the same. You were given a second chance," Martha says, a tear sliding down her beautiful dark skin. "Use it."

"I will, and Maria will get a second chance too," I assure her even though I don't really know.

I just pray she does.

21

JESSE

"How many classes do you have today again?" I ask Emma, who's walking next to me with that damn e-reader in her hand. I look across the quad towards the building of my next class, quietly dreading it. I glance back at my roommate, hoping to see her eyes lift from the device, but they don't.

"Three," she says, still engrossed in her story.

"Do you want to get lunch?"

"Can't. One of my classes runs straight through the lunch hour today. I packed a peanut butter and jelly sandwich."

It's another minute before Emma finally looks up, sighing in relief. She puts the e-reader away and I smile.

"That sucks," I tell her, secretly happy to have her full attention. She nods. "Dinner?"

"That works for me!"

"Alright, I'll see you at six then," Emma says, taking a left towards the science building.

"See you then!" I shout back.

"Yo, Red!" I hear someone yell behind me. Looking around, I don't see any other redheads, so I hesitantly turn around. To my surprise, I see Jesse walking in my direction with some of the guys he'd been with at the café.

He flashes me an apologetic smile.

"Hey, Red," a blond guy says. I think I've seen him before.

"Zoe," Jesse corrects and I give him an amused look.

I did tell him it wasn't an original nickname.

The blond waves him off and extends his hand to me. "I'm Nick."

"I'm Zack," says a redhead standing in the middle of Jesse and Nick.

"Nice to meet you, Red," I say teasingly.

"Touché," he replies with a goofy smile on his face.

I turn my eyes to Jesse. "Hey."

"Hi," he says with an easy smile.

"What are you doing for lunch?" Nick asks, drawing my attention away.

I look at him for a moment too long, trying to figure out why he's asking.

"Will you join us?" Zack adds.

"Who is *us*?" I ask, curiosity getting the better of me. I glance at Jesse to find him looking back at the guys, mouth open.

"Your man Jesse over here," he says pointing at a red-faced Jesse. "Zack and myself, plus a few others," Nick says. I don't register a word after 'your man, Jesse.'

"I'm sure she has better things to do than—" Jesse starts, but I cut him off.

"I'd love to," I answer, looking at Nick and Zack. I can feel Jesse staring at me, but I ignore him. I don't know why he's been so adamant about not letting me meet his friends.

"Great!" replies Zack. "We'll see you at the main dining room at 12pm." He says this matter-of-factly—like we've set up an official appointment.

"See you then," I respond, still refusing to look at Jesse—not out of rebellion, but out of fear.

"See you later then," Jesse says, and my gaze returns to him. He's smiling warmly, and it makes me feel like he actually wants me there. Maybe he wanted it to be my choice.

I look down at my watch, realizing I'm about to be late for class. "Gotta go!" I tell them, waving goodbye. I start walking in the direction of the political science building, feeling my pulse increase, knowing it has nothing to do with being late to class.

It's lunch time and I'm seated at what I now realize is the football team's table. It feels odd sitting here, but at least I'm not the only girl and that makes me feel a little better. I look to my right, to find Jesse smiling back at me. Under the table though, I drum my fingers, the nerves of meeting many of the people Jesse cares about getting the best of me.

I fight through the anxiety though because he cares about them... and I care about him. I just wish people would stop staring at me like I have something stuck in my teeth. *Oh my goodness! Do I?* That would be embarrassing, but also not likely. I haven't eaten anything since I sat down. My salad stares back at me, mocking me. I don't even like salad.

"I can't believe you'd let her meet the guys before meeting us," Mia complains from the other side of the table. I join her in looking at Jesse to find a cute shade of red creeping up his neck. I guess I didn't expect him to be nervous too.

"I didn't mean for her to meet the guys," he argues half- heartedly. "They saw her across the quad."

"It doesn't matter. You shouldn't have kept her from us!" the girl who introduced herself to me as Kaitlyn Hunter shouts from her seat right next to Mia.

I can tell the moment Jesse's about to throw in the towel because of his intake of breath. "I don't know what I was thinking," he says, telling them exactly what they want to hear.

"Neither do I," Kaitlyn shoots back and I laugh. I turn to find Jesse silently begging me for help. I shake my head slightly, telling him he's on his own.

Rolling his eyes at me, we both turn towards Mia and Kaitlyn when one of them clears their throat.

"So, we've got a lot to ask you since we didn't know you existed until five minutes ago," Kaitlyn says, her eyes cutting to Jesse before returning to me.

Oh boy. This will be interesting.

"Ask away," I say, trying to sound as confident as I can. Jesse finds my hand under the table. He squeezes it slightly, giving me the strength I need.

"You just gave the Monster free reign; good luck," Mia warns.

"Hey! I take offense to that. I am *not* a monster!" Kaitlyn replies.

"You know it's all out of love," Mia says, and they both smile at each other.

They continue to tease each other, and I'm happy for the reprieve I'm given. The guys—well Nick—invited me to lunch, and I accepted the invitation right away, but it wasn't until I showed up at the cafeteria and looked at Jesse seated in a table that I realized I was going to meet the girls too.

"Back to you, Zoe; where did you and our Jesse meet?" Kaitlyn asks.

"We met at the hospital," I tell her, and I can see the puzzled look on her face.

"You were an intern there this summer too?" she asks.

I knew this was the kind of question I'd be opening myself to when I answered. I glance at Jesse, but he's still talking to Zack. I shift in my seat, the movement drawing his attention.

Under the table, he puts his hand on my knee. "Everything okay?" he asks quietly.

I nod. "Kaitlyn was just asking where we met."

He stiffens immediately, but I'm not going to lie about this. I squeeze his fingers to tell him as much.

"I wasn't; I was a patient," I respond.

"I'm sorry." Kaitlyn immediately utters her apology, her eyes searching for injuries like everyone does.

I wave it off. "It's all good."

"Have you seen the guys play yet?" Mia asks suddenly, steering the conversation away from me. I give her a slight nod, trying to convey my appreciation to her.

"I haven't. Are they any good?" From the corner of my eye, I see all the guys' heads turn my way.

"Are we any *good*?" Zack asks out loud in mock outrage, causing all the girls to laugh.

I look at him and smile. "Well, are you?" I take advantage of how easy it is to rile him up.

"We're the champions. We have been, and continue to be," he says in a tone that sounds like he's giving a locker room speech before a championship game.

"They're okay," Mia says, earning herself another baffled look from Zack.

"Falcon, you better teach your girl about our greatness," Zack says.

Jesse pats Zack on the shoulder. "Calm down, Hayes."

Mia says, "You should come watch the games with us."

"Sure, I'd love to. Let me know when you girls go and I'll get a ticket." Jesse's told me to go and see his games before, but I haven't taken him up on it yet. I chance another look at him, only to find he's got a goofy smile on his face.

"You don't need to get a ticket. I'll put one, or two if Emma comes, on hold for you," Jesse says in the most tender voice. I bite my lip, feeling myself falling for him a little bit more.

It's only a crush, I reason with myself. He's attractive and kind, and I know I want more than just friendship. Each day, I realize this more and more, but I still don't know if more could happen between us. He hasn't said anything—hinted at anything. He hasn't done anything more than hold my hand and introduce me to his friends—which technically wasn't his choice.

His words make me feel like even though we're in a crowded cafeteria, it's just us. "Thank you. I don't know if Emma will come, but I will."

"Is Emma the other chick we saw you with on the quad and at the cafe?" Zack interrupts with his burger halfway to his mouth.

"Yes, sir; she's the other *chick*," I say emphasizing the last word. I *hate* that word.

Without a care, Zack sinks his teeth into the burger. He chews for a second before saying, "Tell her to stop being lame and come see the best-looking and most skillful team play."

"Lay off, Hayes," a brooding dark-haired guy says, walking towards us with a tray in his hand. He sits down at the end of the table.

"I'll try to convince her," I tell him, knowing it won't be an easy feat.

"That's Chase!" Mia says, introducing me to the newest addition to the table. I catch Kaitlyn rolling her eyes.

I look at him and wave. "I remember him from the café."

"She really did meet everyone before us," Kaitlyn whines, turning accusatory eyes to Jesse again.

Mia laughs. "There's a home game in two weeks. Let's go to that one!" she says, once again changing the direction of the conversation.

"I love that you memorized the game schedule," Zack says, looking all too proud.

"I wonder why," Nick says.

"I remember when Mia sat at *this very* table and told us she didn't care about college football," Zack says. Everyone laughs, all joining together to give Mia a hard time.

"I guess my brother corrected that real quick," Nick says proudly.

"Your brother did what?" someone else says, and I look behind me to find Colton. Even though I've never met him in person, I recognize the most talked about person on campus. He walks to the other side of the table, pushes Nick to the right, and plops down in between him and Mia. Bringing his hand to Mia's chin, he turns her head slightly toward him and places a lingering kiss on her lips. When the kiss finally breaks, he tucks a strand of hair behind her ear, then brings his lips to her forehead.

"Okay, can we please cut that shit out!" Nick says, his face scrunched up in disgust. Everyone dissolves into laughter.

"Stop being jealous," Colton finally says, turning away from Mia and acknowledging everyone's presence.

"Colton, this is Zoe—Jesse's girl," Kaitlyn tells him and the sound of laughter spreads through the table and I know it's because of the song. I sit there awkwardly, not knowing whether to shake Colton's hand or wave. I choose the latter and he nods.

"I wish that I had Jesse's girl," Nick singsongs, and the laughter at the table rises.

Jess gives Nick a stern look. "Shut it."

Nick only grins and continues to hum the tune.

We chat for another half an hour about sports, classes, and the guys—well Zack and Nick mostly—continue to give Jesse a tough time singing the song whenever possible. Slowly the table starts emptying and as it does, I begin to feel lighter. For the first time in a long time, I feel at ease with meeting new people. Although it was terrifying, I did it.

22

ZOE

"Are you sure they'll be okay with me being here?" I ask the moment I reach Jesse in the lobby of my dorm.

When he asked me if I wanted to go out with him this weekend, I was a little surprised, a lot scared, but also really excited. The last time I got to hang out with him, I'd initially felt odd about crashing his lunch, but I still felt like he wanted me there. So, when he texted me this morning, asking if I wanted to go bowling, I jumped at the chance of spending more time with him.

But then he told why we were going bowling, and that everyone else would be there. That's when the panic set in. I had already said yes, so I couldn't back out. And, it's not like I had a bad time the first time around. Still, I asked Emma to come with me, but she turned down my offer, saying she had a research paper to write.

We walk out of the dorm and towards his car which is parked right on the curb. "It'll be fine, Zo. It's not like you haven't met them before. Plus, Kaitlyn and Mia have been asking me about you nonstop since the day they met you," he says, putting me at ease.

"They seem really close," I comment as we reach the passenger side of his car.

Jesse lingers at my side. "Well, they'll soon be sisters-in-law."

My eyes widen. "Colton is going to propose?"

He's gotta be, like, twenty-two!

"Not yet. But not because he doesn't want to. He's hinted at it, but Mia's said something about getting a diploma in her hand before a ring on her finger," he says opening the door for me.

"Smart girl." I'd opt for a diploma first too.

Jesse closes my door and goes around toward the driver side. Getting in and slamming the door after, he finally says, "We all think so."

"They look like they really love each other. At the cafeteria, I noticed he looked at her like she was his whole world."

"That's because to him, she is—Mia, his siblings, and his dad. And well, us too. We're all his family. But Mia, she's the love of his life."

"I can tell. He doesn't seem like a guy who lets people in easily," I say buckling my seatbelt.

"You're right on the money, Red. Colton is pretty closed off, but Mia managed to get in there and pretty quickly at that. She also won over his sister, which is kind of impossible. They even live together now." Jesse looks straight ahead as he turns the key in the ignition and puts the car in drive.

"Mia and Kaitlyn?" I ask.

"Yup. Some girl tried some shady shit last year and Kaitlyn spoke out about it. That got her kicked out of her sorority. She needed a place to live and Mia had an empty room."

"Wow. Can they even kick someone out like that? I mean, aren't there rules against it?" I didn't have the chance to join a sorority when I first started school here. I mean, I didn't want to join anything freshmen year, and sophomore year was cut short so I couldn't. Hearing this though, I'm glad I never had the opportunity.

"I guess she didn't really get kicked out," Jesse clarifies. "The girl, Abbigail, was trying to make Kaitlyn's life a living hell. And before things got worse, Kaitlyn just decided to leave. The new arrangement works well for Mia. It sucks for Colton though," he says with a boyish grin that makes my heart do somersaults. We continue to talk about his friends as we drive over to the bowling alley. I appreciate him telling me about them because it calms my nerves.

"You have interesting friends," I tell him. They're not at all like I expected jocks to be.

He looks at me, grinning, before returning his eyes back to the road. "They're okay."

"So, what's the story with Zack, Nick, and Chase?"

"Zack's really hard-working even though you probably can't tell. He loves girls, flirting, drinking, and partying. Nick, very much like Zack, loves partying. He also really loves the sound of his own voice. Girls love him. He's a bit of a cocky bastard, but not a bad person."

"And Chase?"

"Chase is a mystery. None of us know much about him—I mean except for Colton, who's been his best friend since high school. I went to high school with him too, but we weren't close. Like at all. Chase was always the kid getting into trouble and I wasn't. I played soccer, he played football. Since I've known him, he's always been reserved—dark and mysterious—which I hear girls love, but he doesn't care."

"He doesn't care about the girls?" I ask, digging deeper.

"He likes girls. I've seen him with one here and there, but he's not really trying," he says with a chuckle.

"Huh. Effortlessly charming then?"

"More like girls are attracted to the mysterious bad boy. Some people describe him as the darker version of Colton."

"Is that so?"

"Yeah, I mean... I get why."

"I see that too."

"Where's this sudden interest in the guys coming from anyway?" he asks, looking straight ahead. "Do you like one of them?" he questions coming to a stop at a red light. His eyes find mine, genuine concern reflected in their blue depths.

Is he jealous?

The light turns green, and he focuses back on the road. I watch as his hands tighten on the steering wheel, and he swallows a few times. The silence in the car is almost unbearable.

In a surprising gesture, he slowly reaches over and takes my hand in his. Carefully—curiously—he entwines his fingers with mine, and I immediately feel goose bumps spread over my body.

This is new.

We've never held hands like this before and it feels like more confirmation that there's more than innocent friendship here. I just wish he'd come out and say it.

"You're not interested in any of them, not even a little?" he presses.

My breathing hitches in my throat, the feel of his fingers caressing mine just too distracting. "I'm not interested in *them*," I whisper, staring at him, hoping he can read between the lines.

His fingers tighten. "Good," he says. He slows the car and pulls into the parking lot of the bowling alley. After putting the car in park and shutting off the engine, we sit in silence, the air still tense. The words we want to say to each other are on the tips of our tongues, our hands still intertwined, but our courage lacking.

Tap. Tap. Tap.

We're startled by the sound of Zack tapping on Jesse's window. We let go of each other like we've just been caught doing something we shouldn't have.

Zack opens the driver's side door. "Could you come in already? You two can do this lovey shit later!" He cackles, ruffling Jesse's hair like an annoying big brother.

"Dude, seriously?" Jesse asks, flustered as he pushes Zack away. While they bicker back and forth, I open my door and slide out of the passenger seat, giving myself a second to catch my breath before joining the boys at the entrance of the bowling alley.

"Ready?" Jesse asks.

"Yeah, ready to lose?" Zack jumps in obnoxiously.

"I'm ready... to win, that is," I say, opening the door and stepping inside.

JESSE

I WALK INTO THE BOWLING ALLEY WITH ZACK ON MY RIGHT, AND ZOE hiding somewhere on my left. Something shifted in our relationship, but before we could figure out what that change was, Zack had screwed it up. We head straight towards the lane where Nick, Chase, Kaitlyn, Mia, and Colton are gathered. Seeing them all in a group, laughing together, I can see why Zoe was nervous to come. Maybe it's our sheer size, or the fact that we play football, and that alone—in this town at least—makes us visible.

Still, I want her to be here, to hang out with everyone—because she's one of us now, whether she knows it or not.

"Ready to get your ass handed to you?" Nick asks, high-fiving Zack. I roll my eyes at their assholery. It's like they're the same person.

"I see you brought another loser with you." Nick directs his statement at Zoe, whose hazel eyes light up in defiance.

"Dude, cut it out!" Mia shouts from her place next to Colton. Colton looks back and forth between Mia and an open-mouthed Nick and smiles.

"Nick talks a lot, but his game is lacking," Kaitlyn jumps in, adding wood to the fire.

"All bark, no bite. I see!" Zoe mocks and the sound of laughter echoes around the room.

And she's in.

Just. Like. That.

"Where's the birthday boy?" Zack asks, amidst the laughter.

"Birthday boy? The last time I checked, I was a man,"

I look over my shoulder to find Blake and Kiya, their hands twisted together just as mine and Zoe's had been a few minutes ago.

"And the last time I checked, he was all man too," Kiya says and I see Blake stand a little taller. Once again, laughter erupts.

With pride in his eyes, Blake kisses Kiya on the cheeks and adds, "Damn right."

"Man, you're softening up," Zack whines with a drink in his hand. When the heck did that happen?

"What do you mean?" Mia asks, running over to her best friend and giving her a hug that has Kiya gasping for air. If you see the way Mia clings to her, you'd think they haven't seen each other in years instead of a couple of months.

"I mean, Blake and Kiya, you and Colton, and now Jesse and Zoe," Zack says, pointing at each of us.

"*Us?*" I ask.

"You guys are dating? It's about time dude!" Blake says, bringing his hand in the air for a high five I leave unanswered.

"I *knew* it! I can't believe you didn't tell us!" Kaitlyn squeals at a visibly uncomfortable Zoe. All eyes watch us as they wait for confirmation of our relationship status.

When I look at a reddening Zoe, I realize it's my fault they're confused. I've been spending a lot of time with her. I've brought her around twice. Why wouldn't I, though? She's my friend.

A friend whose hand I hold.

Whose smile causes me to smile in return.

Whose laughter is music to my ears.

Whose absence I feel and whose presence I cherish.

Yep, a *friend*. That's all she is.

"Quit making it awkward," Mia states, attempting to save us from further scrutiny.

"Didn't we come here to celebrate a birthday?" Kiya says, following Mia's lead and moving the conversation along.

I steal a glance at Zoe, who looks nervous and I wish I could make it better.

Shit.

I'm all over the place.

No wonder my friends are confused—I'm confused too.

23

ZOE

I keep putting myself in less than ideal situations. I realize that now. Ever since that whole 'are you guys dating' misunderstanding at bowling last weekend, you'd think I'd have learned my lesson and stayed away... Nope. No such luck.

Instead, I'm walking towards the box office of the stadium, getting ready to watch my first college football game. I'm going to cheer on Jesse while I sit next to his friends.

I should stop hanging out with them altogether—I wanted to after I saw the look on Jesse's face when his friends insinuated we were dating. Then again, he didn't deny it either.

"Over here!" I hear someone yell the moment I reach the ticket window. I turn to find Mia and Kaitlyn standing close to security. Both of them are wearing team jerseys, and for a second, I wish I'd bought one too. Instead, I'm wearing a flowy blue shirt. They can't say I don't have school spirit, right?

I walk over to where they're standing, relieved they spotted me so soon. "Hi."

Mia greets me with a comforting hug, followed by Kaitlyn's own embrace. "I'm so glad you found the right place," Mia says.

I looked around at the sea of blue and white—the colors of Bragan University's Lions. The air is buzzing and the enthusiasm is palpable. "I am too," I reply. I could've so easily gotten lost in this crowd.

"Plus, it's about time you decided to spend some girl time with us," Kaitlyn adds with a hint of mischief in her eyes.

"Should I be afraid?" I ask jokingly, but also not really. I can already tell she's a handful.

"Be afraid. Be very afraid," Mia says her face serious before she starts laughing.

"Are you quoting movies now?" I ask, chuckling.

"Wow, everyone really knows that line! I said that to Colton the first time he came over," she says with a smile that appears the moment she mentions her boyfriend's name.

Kaitlyn makes a gagging noise. "Can we stop talking about my brother? It's enough that I walk in to find you guys making out on the couch all the time. By the way, I think that couch needs to be burned!"

Mia's face reddens. "Sorry! We get too lost in the moment sometimes."

"I don't know how much more of this sweetness I can deal with."

"Hey!" Mia exclaims. "It is not that bad! Look, we'll try and keep it in the bedroom," she adds, still red of embarrassment.

"Please," Kaitlyn pleads and I laugh.

"So where do we go?" I ask as people with blue-and-white painted faces sing and chant.

"We have tickets being held for us at the box office," Mia informs me.

"Tickets the players put aside for their girlfriends," Kaitlyn adds, and I wonder if sisters of players can also get in, or if she's dating someone on the team.

"For their families, actually," Mia clarifies, answering my question before I have a chance to ask.

I'm eager to watch Jesse in action. I haven't seen him at all this week and I don't like how that feels. I understand he's had class and practice though.

"Just so you know, after you watch the game from the box, you'll never want to be a regular spectator again," Mia warns me as we walk back to get our tickets. Let's hope it's not something I get used to because I'm not sure it's something that'll last.

"Will I be okay to head in? I mean, I'm not family or..." I pause, then add painfully, 'a player's *girlfriend*.' And I didn't buy my own ticket.

"Don't worry. Jesse's got you."

That he does.

The problem is, I don't know if I have him.

MIA WAS RIGHT ABOUT THE BOX SEATS. THE VIEW IS AMAZING. FROM where I'm sitting, I can see the entire field, yet it still feels like I'm up close and personal. I really should've come to watch a game earlier.

Our players run around in their baby blue and white uniforms, all their extra armor making them look like giants. I scan the players' backs, searching for the number Jesse told me he'd be wearing—number three. When he called last night, he told me to look out for him—that he'd be looking out for me too.

By halftime, our team is down ten points. Mia takes some time to explain all the technical aspects of the game to me during the break, and I'm surprised at the level of investment I'm putting into this sport.

"A touchdown and a field goal are all they needed to tie the game!" Mia frantically says.

"And two touchdowns will seal the deal?" I ask, absorbing her excitement.

"Yes!" she says before turning her attention back to the field as the players walk toward the locker rooms. She's tense, and I understand why. She's been sitting here watching the other team try and sack or tackle her man. Luckily for all of us, it's only happened once so far because, despite how much the other team keeps trying, Colton somehow keeps finding a way to avoid the blitz.

"I'm grabbing snacks," Kaitlyn announces. "Do you guys want anything?" She doesn't seem too interested in the game; she's spent most of her time firing out text messages.

"Coke and popcorn please," Mia answers with a smile.

"I'll take a Coke, too," I add. With the way I've been joining Mia in shouting at whatever is happening on the field, my throat is dry.

"I can come with you if you want?" Mia says to an already retreating Kaitlyn.

"All good," Kaitlyn replies, rushing out the door. Mia frowns.

"She doesn't like football?" I ask.

"She likes it...I think. She's been coming to every game with me, but she always disappears at halftime though."

Huh, interesting. I wonder where she goes.

"She probably just needs a break from the intensity of the game," Mia says but, somehow, I doubt that's the answer.

"So, I take it you're a huge football fan?" I say, making small talk.

She nods. "I always have been—mostly professional, but now I'm more of a Colton fan than anything else," she says with a grin, and I wonder if they can get any cuter. Seriously.

I level her with a serious stare. "So, should I be worried about us not winning?"

"We should be good. We always are." She's confident, which makes me believe every word.

"So," she says, pausing a moment, "Tell me about you and Jesse?"

"I'm not sure there's much to tell," I answer honestly. Maybe Mia will be able to help me figure out what's running through his mind.

She looks at me skeptically. "I'm sure there is."

"We've just become really good friends." *Although I want more*, I add silently.

"This summer, while he was an intern at the hospital?" I nod. "I can tell, you know?" she says sweetly.

"Can tell, what?" I ask, knowing exactly what she means, but waiting for her to put into words what I've felt this whole time.

She takes a deep breath. "I can tell you like him."

For some reason, I still try to deny it. "I don't—"

"You don't have to lie," she says gently. "I won't say anything." Silently, I debate whether I should just come clean. Looking into her almond-shaped brown eyes, I see genuine kindness there. From the little time I've known her, I can tell she's honest, caring, and someone who could be a good friend, so I take a chance on her. It's all about taking chances, especially when you've been given a second one.

"Is it that obvious?" I ask, mortified at the thought that I've been so transparent when it comes to Jesse. Then again, if it's that obvious, why hasn't he noticed?

"Not to others. Well, to Kaitlyn too, but we're girls. We pick up on these things."

I sigh, praying Mia answers my follow up question in the negative. "And the guys have no idea?"

"I don't know. It's hard to tell with them. When Colton and I started hanging out more, they started picking up on it and teasing us. But it's different with Jesse."

"Different, how?" I ask.

"He's just different. He's been through a lot. I mean Colton has too, but it's just different," Mia says and right as I'm about to ask what he's been through, a worried-looking Kaitlyn walks into the room with two Cokes, and popcorn.

"Everything okay?" Mia asks her, meeting her halfway to take the drinks.

"Yeah, all good. Just some assholes outside."

"Did you give them a good dose of Kaitlyn? Are they still there?"

"They're gone now. Don't worry."

Mia hands me my drink. "Thank you, Kaitlyn," I tell her.

She gives me a smile. "Any time Zoe. You're one of us now." She says this like it's a given, and while to her it may not mean much, it does to me.

After spending this time with them, I've felt like I could truly be good friends with these girls.

Together, we watch the second half. This time, we cheer instead of yell. Apparently, the Bragan Lions are nicknamed the Comeback Team, because whenever they come back after halftime, they always win. Mia, Kaitlyn, and I scream in celebration while the guys revel in their win on the field.

24

ZOE

"Doesn't throwing parties get old, or at least tiring?" I ask Jesse as I tentatively start walking towards him. He opens his arms and embraces me. I look around the Football House—his home. The last time he invited me to a party, I'd said no, but as the weeks go by, it gets harder to pass up an opportunity to spend time with him. Tonight, they're celebrating yet another amazing win. According to Mia, it's because they have the best quarterback, kicker, and overall team in the league. All that they do is destroy the competition on the field.

I can't believe they thought having a post-win celebration party was a good idea. Last year, the parties started towards the end of the season. Now, there's a party practically every weekend. Jesse tried to explain that having these parties motivate the guys– something about alcohol, girls, and ego stroking being good for them.

Shrugging, he says, "Tiring, yes, but people keep coming back. So,

I've got no choice but to play the welcoming host. Come on." He takes my hand and guides me further inside.

This team has won every game since the National Championship —at least that's what I'm told. And while I love that they're so good, I also know the team's success is part of the reason I barely get to see Jesse anymore. Between his extra difficult classes, football practices and games, I only catch glimpses of him as he runs to the field, or on those random occasions that he shows up at my dorm.

At his insistence, and with a small push from Kaitlyn and Mia, I finally gave into the pressure and decided to come and celebrate.

We stop when a blond-haired guy high fives Jesse. "Jesse, good game, bro!"

"Yeah, well done!" a brunette echoes. There's something about the way she says it that gets on my nerves. I watch her every move intently, seeing the way her eyes flicker to me briefly before turning back to him. But when she runs her fingers up his arm, an unnecessary anger rises within me, and I want to slap her hand away.

"Thanks," he responds casually and immediately moves away. I smile. Good riddance.

We continue to zig zag through the crowds, his hand still holding mine. "Where are we going?" I ask.

He turns his head, his lips mere inches from my own. "What?"

"Where are we going?" I repeat, but I whisper the question in his ear, finding myself suddenly out of breath.

He leans in closer. This time, he's the one who whispers in my ear. "We're going to the backyard. It's quieter out there."

I lick my lips, lost in his nearness. "Okay."

He tucks a strand of my short hair back behind my ear, his eyes firmly fixed on my own. "Come on." Tugging me closer, her wraps his arm around my waist, and I suddenly feel…complete.

We walk through the kitchen and out the back door into an ample yard.

"You guys are freaking adorable," Kaitlyn says. I shake my head at her comment, knowing if it weren't dark outside, they'd see me blush.

Jesse leads us over to where Kaitlyn, Colton, Mia, and Chase are lounging in front of the fire.

"I knew I'd find you guys out here," Jesse says, leading me to an empty chair and taking the one next to me.

"Apparently, that's what these two do," Kaitlyn answers, pointing at Colton and Chase.

"I did not expect to see *you* sitting out here instead of partying tonight, Kaitlyn," Jesse says.

"Sometimes you gotta take a night off. Plus, it's nice out here," she answers. We all sit around silently for a few seconds, and it's unbelievable how different it is out here than in there.

"It's a little weird that you guys throw parties and then leave the house," I finally say out loud.

"Well, Colton apparently enjoys coming out here to cool off," Mia says, giving Colton a knowing look. He shakes his head but smiles back at her.

"Mia doesn't like parties and loves Colton," Kaitlyn adds, shrugging.

"Kaitlyn is taking a brief time out from parties," Mia states, and I laugh at how they're answering for each other.

"Because you dared me to!" Kaitlyn chimes in.

"Because I dared her to," Mia echoes.

"Really? A dare to stop going to parties?" I ask.

Kaitlyn conspiratorially whispers, "Mia doesn't think I can turn down a good party. My intent is to prove her wrong,"

"Okay, Zoe, last fall, my first introduction to Kaitlyn was her throwing up on the side walk outside a bar," Mia says, her face scrunching up in disgust. I laugh.

"Need I remind you that if it wasn't for my drunk ass, you wouldn't have met my brother," Kaitlyn returns, not in the least bothered by Mia ratting her out.

"True, but there's no need for your drunk ass to introduce me to anyone else."

"Damn right," Colton says, tuning into the conversation.

"Chase here just doesn't like people," Kaitlyn says, jabbing her thumb in his direction. I still don't know much about him except that he doesn't say much and he's a savage on the field. I watch him to see if he's going to bite back at the jab, but he only looks at Kaitlyn for a minute too long, then shifts his focus back to the beer in his hand.

"Jesse, why are you out here?" Mia asks, trying to fill the silence.

"It's too loud inside," he responds.

Kaitlyn snorts. "Really? It has nothing to do with wanting to spend some alone time with a certain someone?"

Freaking Kaitlyn and her overt comments making me blush all over again.

"If that had been my intention, I clearly failed since you're all out here too," Jesse retorts.

Kaitlyn stands up and grabs a beer from a cooler. "I'm bored.

Can we at least play *Never Have I Ever*?"

"Pass," Colton replies immediately.

"Could you just give it a try?" she begs her brother.

"Nope," he replies, popping the *p*. Kaitlyn rolls her eyes in response.

Giving up on convincing Colton, Kaitlyn turns to the rest of us. "Anyone else want to play?"

"I'm down," Mia answers, shaking her head at Colton.

"Me too," I reply since no one else is jumping at the opportunity.

"I'm game," Jesse follows, and I smile. Then I look at Mia who glares at Colton.

"Fine, I'll play too," he grumbles, and I work hard to hold back my laughter.

"Do you wanna play?" Kaitlyn asks, directing her question at Chase.

He's staring at the fire, and for a second, I think he won't even give her a response. "I'm good," he finally says.

"Of course you are," she says, annoyed.

"Who starts?" Mia asks, eager to redirect the conversation. She does that a lot when things start to get weird.

"You can. I think you're the only one excited to play," Kaitlyn tells her.

"Do we say things we didn't do and see if someone else has done it?" I ask, trying to get some clarification.

"Yeah," Kaitlyn confirms.

"Okay, never have I ever..." Mia pauses briefly, mulling her statement over, "...gotten black-out drunk," she says, pointing directly at Kaitlyn and laughing.

"Thanks," Kaitlyn says sarcastically as takes a sip of her drink. Jesse goes to the cooler, grabbing a beer for himself and one for me.

"My turn! Never have I ever been in love," Kaitlyn says. Mia and Colton drink at the same time while making eyes at each other. Cuteness overload. I've never been in love so I don't drink. I turn to Jesse just in time to see him take a sip of his own and I can't help being surprised. I wonder who he was in love with? I wonder what happened? I shift uncomfortably. I guess I don't know him as well as I thought—and I don't like how that feels.

Chase stands up abruptly, grabbing another beer. He opens the bottle and tosses it back. I don't know if it's just bad timing, or if he's answering the question.

"You've never been in love?" Mia asks Kaitlyn.

"Why are you so shocked? I'm still young. Plus, you've never been black-out drunk," Kaitlyn responds.

"My turn," I say. "Never have I ever had my heart broken." I say following the same line of questioning because I'm eager to learn more about Jesse. Kaitlyn chugs her beer and so does Jesse. "Sorry," I tell them, realizing I shouldn't have gone there.

"Not your fault," Kaitlyn answers, taking another drink for good measure.

"Never have I ever made out with a stranger!" Kaitlyn calls out.

"Okay, game over!" Colton says, stopping his sister.

"Is that a yes, bro?" Kaitlyn teases.

Mia pokes him. "Oh, no way. Why do you want to end the game?"

"I don't want to know if you've ever made out with a damn stranger," he states matter-of-factly.

"More like you don't want to admit that you've made out with a stranger," she says.

. . .

THE GAME FINISHES AFTER COLTON'S OUTBURST AND THE REST OF THE night is spent a lot differently than I expected when I agreed to come to the party. Instead of dealing with drunks and seeing a bunch of girls parade themselves around Jesse, we just hang out outside with a nice breeze and a fire. We talk for what's probably hours— well mostly Mia and I chat; the guys are happy just to watch it happen. And despite only meeting Kaitlyn and Mia a few weeks ago, I feel like we've known each other for a lifetime.

I look around at the group of people who have quickly become my friends, noting the absent way both Kaitlyn and Chase are staring into the fire. Chase has barely spoken a word all night, but I've still noticed the way he looks at Kaitlyn when he thinks nobody's watching. It makes me wonder if there's something else going on there.

I steal a glance at Mia, who's shifted from her chair to Colton's lap. His strong arms are wrapped around her, his nose buried in her dark hair.

Swoon.

I find myself wishing I had what they do.

Finally, I look at Jesse to find him already looking at me. He gives me a sweet smile which I return. His hand finds mine once again, and we don't let go until the party ends. We don't let go until everyone's gone home and we're the only ones left outside.

25

ZOE

"Thanks for coming!" I throw my arm over my roommate's shoulder and awkwardly embrace her.

"I'll try anything once," Emma says. "Plus, isn't this a rite of passage or something?" she asks as we follow the masses on our way to one of the last football games of the season.

"*Anything*?" I ask.

"Not *every*thing. Some things," she corrects.

"You should be thanking me for enabling you to have a proper college experience!"

"Not a chance," Emma says, stopping to put her hair in a ponytail.

"You couldn't find a blue shirt?" I ask, pointing at her black shirt and jeans. "Couldn't have a little team spirit?"

She hitches a hand onto one hip. "I'm missing out on some serious reading time here. For *you*. Don't push it."

I try to hide my grin. "I'll make it worth your while. Jesse got us an extra ticket so you can watch from the box!"

"What box?" she asks, looking disinterested as she avoids bumping into a group of drunk college students in front of us.

"Wow, how clueless are you?" I tell her acting like I've known all about the perks of box seats. Truly, if it weren't for Kaitlyn and Mia, I'd be sitting somewhere in the bleachers.

"I didn't think you were a football aficionado, Zoe."

"Me neither," I say honestly.

"Oh, so it's basically something we have to do because of your ginormous crush on Jesse?"

"We don't have to do it. I want to." That's the only thing I counter with. I want to be here. "We get to watch from a viewing box that sits on the fifty-yard line, and just outside the doors are the snacks," I explain.

"Cool," she says, devoid of any enthusiasm.

We walk into the stadium and I head over to the box office like I have a few times before. Telling the attendant my name and showing her my student ID, she gives me the tickets and we head upstairs. I'm grateful Jesse got one of his teammates to get him a ticket so Emma could join. She's become a really good friend and I want her to experience this. I think she'll enjoy it despite her hesitance.

Exiting the elevator, we open the door to the box where I know the girls are waiting. The moment we walk inside, I'm greeted by a few familiar faces. Who would've thought that I'd be coming to games so often that people would know who I am? That may also be a side-effect of hanging out with Jesse.

At the back of the room, which is the closest to the field, I spot two Hunter jerseys, both with different numbers. Quarterback and tight end—the Hunter brothers. I know exactly who's wearing them too; Mia supporting her boyfriend, and Kaitlyn supporting her twin brother.

I greet Mia and Kaitlyn, who immediately get up. Mia embraces me and Kaitlyn does the same.

"Zoe! You made it!" Mia exclaims, perpetually bubbly.

"I wouldn't miss it for the world. This is one of the final games!"

I'm shocked at my own excitement and ever-growing knowledge of the sport.

"I'm so glad Mia found another football lover. That way, I don't have to feign interest," Kaitlyn says.

"Shut up. You like football," Mia teases.

"Oh, guys, this is Emma," I say, introducing my roommate who remains a few steps behind me, using me as a shield.

"Hi Emma, I'm Mia and this is Kaitlyn," Mia says with a warm smile.

"We've heard a lot about you." Kaitlyn adds this in a creepy tone.

Emma groans. "Oh, God, what did she say?"

We all laugh.

"All good things, don't worry. We already like you. You're going to have to tell me about those romance books you read," Mia replies, and I can see Emma turning red.

My roommate looks at me accusingly. "You told her about those?"

I shrug. "They had to know why you never come out with me. I told them you lived in a literary world."

"We should have a book club!" Mia suggests out of nowhere.

Kaitlyn looks like she's been given the worst offer of her life. "Hard pass. I'm not reading for fun."

"I'm with Kaitlyn on this one. No, thank you," I echo.

"Ignore them," Mia says. "I'll read with you. When you start reading the next book, tell me what it is and I'll download it too. I need some fun reading before I graduate and have to be an adult." She sits down beside Kaitlyn and I take the next seat.

"Sounds good," Emma replies, sitting next to me.

THIS GAME IS SHIT. THE TEAM WE'RE PLAYING AGAINST KEEPS MAKING really questionable plays and the referees aren't doing anything about it.

And we're losing.

I guess at some point every team loses, but this has been a perfect season so far. We have won every game—both home and away—but judging by the way things are looking, our streak may end tonight.

"Seriously!" Mia yells, pointing at the field when the defense runs through the o-line and sacks Colton. He gets up slowly and I swear he looks in the direction of our box. I can imagine him searching for Mia to assure her he's okay. She yells expletives at the refs and the other team as she sticks up for her boyfriend. She's even yelling at our own team to get it together. On the other hand, there's Kaitlyn and Emma. Kaitlyn sits more quietly than usual, and Emma has her e-reader out as she devours her latest read. I shake my head.

"Whatcha reading?" I ask her.

"Sports romance," she says, never lifting her eyes from her reader.

I watch the teams switch at the beginning of the third quarter. "What sport?"

"Football," she says and I laugh.

"You're seriously at a football game reading a book about football?" She says surprised.

"Football in books is better," she answers matter-of-factly, her eyes returning to her screen.

I turn back to the field and spot Jesse getting ready for the kick off. I watch as he takes measured steps away from the ball and I can tell he's counting each of them. Although the helmet and distance prevent me from seeing the determination in his eyes, I know it's there.

He runs towards the football, picking up speed as he gets closer until his right foot makes contact with the ball, sending it flying to the other side of the field. It's a perfect kick, landing just outside the end zone. The receiver on the opposing team catches the ball and begins to run, gaining yardage with every step. One of our players tries to stop him, but misses the tackle by mere inches and crashes into the ground. Their kick returner runs to his own thirty-yard line, continuing down the field with the football safely in his arms.

Mia is on her feet, yelling for someone to do something, to stop them from getting closer to the end zone, scoring and destroying our undefeated season. I rise to my feet as well when another tackle is missed and the player continues past the fifty- yard line. He reaches our forty when from out of nowhere, I see Jesse running toward him.

"Come on!" I scream as I wait for him to take down the player. He reaches him, his hands going to the player's jersey, and in a swift motion, pulling the other guy towards him and down. They both crash to the ground, the ball knocked loose. Jesse rises from the ground rapidly, throwing himself on top of the ball.

"A fumble and a recovery!" the announcer states, and even Kaitlyn gets up and screams in excitement along with Mia and me.

JESSE'S PLAY WAS GAME-CHANGING—THE ONE THAT TRANSFORMED everything. By the time the fourth quarter starts, we're only down by six since the previous team missed the extra point. Our team moves the chains and find themselves at the fifty-yard line. When Mia finally settles back down, she explains that this was the team that almost blew us out of the water last time.

Another spectacular play gets us closer to the end zone.

"Okay, so it's third and three, and they're on the thirty-five-yard line. If they don't convert then we lose," Mia says out loud to no one in particular.

"Let's hope they can do it," I respond since aside from her, I'm the only one from our group paying attention to the game. The team comes back from the time out they'd called and take their positions on the field. Colton makes the call and the ball is snapped to him. He surveys the field, looking for the open player but as he searches, a player from the other side gets through the o-line and runs straight toward him. Instantly, I see Zack heading toward Colton. He makes an incredible tackle, bringing down the rusher and allowing Colton to have more time in the pocket to pass the ball.

Colton looks around the field once more, sending the ball flying over to number 87, Nick, who makes the catch and begins to run. Nick holds the ball as the other team's players run toward him. Nick, however, is quicker on his feet, maneuvering so swiftly that the other player trips and falls. This allows Nick to move closer and closer to the end zone. We're all back on our feet, chanting his name and praying for the touchdown that will help us finally tie the game.

Twenty yards. Ten yards. Inches. And he's in!

"Yes!" Mia and I scream out loud, and to my surprise, Kaitlyn once gets to her feet and cheers for her brother. Family over everything, right?

I turn to Emma, who I find looking up from her e-reader and down at the field with an expression of awe.

"You saw that?" I ask.

She nods. "That was pretty cool."

"Better than the games in your book?"

"Don't push it," she says with a smile. She puts her reader in her bag and I know that the game has finally captured her full attention.

Jesse takes the field again, lining up to go for extra point. The players get in position, the ball is snapped and Jesse kicks it flawlessly. I follow it as it goes through the center of the goal post. When I bring my eyes back to where Jesse is standing, I find him sprawled on the ground.

"What happened?" I demand, a bad feeling creeping its way through my body.

"A player tackled him after he kicked," Emma responds.

"Roughing the kicker, Ref! Roughing the kicker!" Mia shouts and I stay seated—not because I don't want to join her in yelling, but because Jesse is still on the ground and my legs are frozen. My heart is beating erratically, just waiting for a sign that he's okay.

I hold my breath, but nothing happens. The coaches rush to the field and the players surround him, blocking him from my view. I keep my hand on my chest and while I wait, my mind wanders to the hospital. I think about Jesse's love of football. I think about all the pain he must be feeling right now. All the bones that he could have possibly broken. With each thought, my heart breaks more and more for him. A tear slides down my face and I let it fall.

"He's getting up," Mia says, her hand on my shoulder as she brings me back from my parade of horrors. I breathe a sigh of relief and watch Jesse nod his head, reassuring people that he's okay. I get up, joining Mia and the whole stadium in cheering for him he walks, unaided, to the sideline.

"Thank God," I mutter.

"I know how it feels," Mia says. "Trust me. Colton has had a few horrible sacks and I've wanted to make my way down there to make sure he's okay, and then find the player that hurt my man." She has a fierce look in her eyes that tells me she isn't kidding.

I nod in agreement because she's right. That's exactly how I felt, but I don't know if it's how I should feel.

Mia and Colton—they're a forever thing.

They're together.

Jesse and me.

There isn't an *us*.

At least, not yet.

26

ZOE

"Thanks for coming with me," I say, turning to look at Emma, who still seems a little awestruck. She pushes her glasses up a little higher on her nose as she walks into the Football House beside me. She might be uncomfortable, but she's here because I asked her to come—especially since we both skipped the celebration party last time, choosing to hang out at the dorm instead.

"Don't mention it. Two hours though—that's all I'm giving you," she says sternly, like a mother reminding her child of their curfew.

"Yes, Mom," I joke.

"Look, you don't have to leave with me. You can stay." She points at herself. "Me? I'm definitely going to go."

I smile at her, then look up to see the house ahead of us. Some may call me a bad influence for dragging her away from her books and fictional characters and into the madness with me, but I'm okay with that. I just want her to live a little more too, like I am.

Last week, as much as I wanted to run over to the House after the game and make sure Jesse was okay, I didn't. I already knew he was fine. I just needed time to process the reason *why* I'd felt the way I did when he was hurt—space to think about how I *really* feel about him.

This week though, I decided to come to the party despite my reservations, because when it comes to Jesse, I can't stay away for too long. I haven't talked to him in the last couple of days, and I feel off-kilter because of it. He doesn't know I'm coming either, so I hope he likes surprises.

We've just stepped onto the front path when a shirtless guy races past us, nearly knocking Emma over. I pull her out of the way just in time.

"Seriously, why do people even find parties appealing?" she says, glaring at the rowdy crowd.

I grab her hand and enter through the front door. "Free beer?" I answer heading straight to the kitchen so that we can grab some drinks.

Going straight to one of the coolers, I grab a can of beer, pouring it into a red cup. I offer it to Emma, but she scrunches her nose. "Beer is gross. I prefer wine."

"You're an old soul. Wine and books."

She sighs blissfully. "Wine and books are literally life."

"Well, there's no wine here so you'll have to lower your standards for tonight."

"Seriously?" she asks, and I think she's outraged at the lack of wine.

I laugh. "Let loose for the next two hours. Drink some beer, have fun, then you can escape to your fictional world."

"Define let loose..."

"Dance with me?"

"Nope, not happening."

"Come on," I insist, grabbing her hand and walking us over to the living room where bodies are pressed against each other, moving out of sync to the weird mix that's playing.

She fights me every step of the way. "I don't wanna! I don't dance! Why don't you go find Jesse!"

"I came here with you—not him," I remind her. Although he's definitely the reason I showed up.

"But you came here for him," she says, reading my thoughts.

"No, I didn't."

"Don't lie to yourself," Emma shouts over the music. "You know that's why we're here."

"We're just here to enjoy the party—to live a little," I add.

"So, you're saying it has nothing to do with the fact that you spend your every free moment with Jesse?"

"I spend my time with you!"

She gives me a look I can only interpret as incredulity. "You have this last week, which makes me suspicious."

"Emma, I *like* spending time with you."

"You also like spending time with him. A couple of weeks ago, you guys were at the hospital together."

"We were visiting Maria, so that doesn't count."

"Okay, and what about the day after that?"

Dammit!

"I ran an errand with him. He wanted someone to accompany him to the store."

"And the day after that one?"

"Okay! I know where you're going with this. Maybe I have been spending a lot of time with him, but that's what you do with friends. I've spent the last week nagging you to do stuff with me."

"Just friends, huh? At least for now."

Her unfinished statement hangs over my head, because she's right —I don't want to just be his friend. I want so much more.

"You haven't been spending time with him this week, though."

"Nope," I reply. I've barely spoken to him at all. When he messaged me, I told him I wanted to spend some time with Emma. That was my excuse, and I think he bought it.

"I haven't seen him here either. I've been trying to find him so I can hand you off to him and finally make my escape," she says candidly and I laugh. I know Jesse is probably outside in the backyard with the others, but I don't want to go out there unless he takes me.

My favorite song starts playing. "Wow, I see what kind of friend you are. Now stop distracting me with conversation. We've gotta dance!" I grab her hand, forcing her to move to the music.

"Okay, my two hours are up!" Emma says as the song we're dancing to comes to an end.

Surprisingly, she's loosened up a lot, but I think it was less me and more the random bottle of white wine we were able to find in the fridge.

"Has it been two hours already?" I ask. It doesn't really feel like it.

"Yes, ma'am; I timed it."

I chuckle. "Of course you did."

"Are you staying?" she asks. I chance another look around like I've been doing every five minutes for the last two hours, and still no luck. Jesse's nowhere in sight.

I didn't talk to him during today's game, or after. He didn't even send me a message about winning. It's been radio-silence from him and it feels odd.

I really want to see him tonight but I guess that's not happening.

"I'll come with," I tell Emma, and I can't hide the disappointment in my voice.

She searches my eyes. "Are you sure?"

"Yeah, I'm good. I think we've celebrated enough." And so has everyone else. I swear everyone's at this party...everyone but the one I really wanted to see.

"Okay, let's go home!"

We make a beeline for the exit, bumping and running into a few people on the way. Right before reaching the door, the same shirtless guy from earlier runs straight into Emma, soaking her with the pitcher of beer he's carrying.

"Shit, I'm sorry," the guy slurs, clearly intoxicated.

"It's okay," Emma says, reminding me of how sweet she is. Any other girl would have likely lashed out, but not my roommate.

"The bathroom's upstairs if you need it," he says, looking genuinely apologetic. "I'm so sorry again."

Emma looks to me "It is okay if we go to the bathroom before heading out?"

"Yes! I'll come with." We zig zag our way back through the masses and head to the stairs. When we reach the landing, we ask a few people for directions to the bathroom before someone finally tells us where it is.

"I'll wait for you out here," I tell Emma who runs in the moment the door opens and another girl walks out.

"Thanks," she says, pushing her glasses up on her face before shutting the door.

I lean against the opposite wall, waiting for Emma to finish up, getting lost in the buzz of voices.

"I haven't seen Jesse tonight, have you?"

The mention of Jesse's name causes me to turn my head to where I find two girls near the stairs with red cups in their hands. There's a blonde girl, and a brunette, both wearing Greek letters on their shirts.

"Me neither! I was looking forward to hooking up with him!" the brunette says, and I'm consumed with anger just as quickly as the words leave her mouth. I love how she casually says, 'hooking up with him' like he'd just sleep with her. I don't think he's the type to do something like that…at least, I hope he isn't.

I wonder what makes her think he would?

Girl, breathe. It's not your place, I remind myself.

"Isn't he dating someone?" says the blonde and I smile.

"There's a rumor he's been hanging out with this girl who just started school. She's got cancer or some shit."

The smile falls from my face in a heartbeat. I didn't think people knew. Maybe they remember me from when I started school, but had to leave?

"Seriously? I heard the last girl he dated had cancer too. She died though. Does he have a thing for cancer patients?"

"Maybe he likes projects," her friend says. "He seems like the kind of guy who likes charity work."

My rage intensifies.

I want to go over there and hit her. I hate the way she's talking about people with cancer—as if they're projects, or pariahs—like we are nothing but misfortunate people.

"She's not even pretty. I doubt he's dating her. He's probably just entertaining her because she reminds him of his ex," the blonde says, flipping her hair over her shoulder.

"You're right. I'd say go for it. He won't turn you down, especially not for a girl like that."

A girl like *what*? She has no idea what I look like. If she did, I doubt she'd be talking about me while I stand mere feet away.

I'm seconds away from putting them in their place when I feel someone grasp my hand. Looking up, my eyes connect with Emma's. By the concern there, she must've heard everything that was just said.

"Ignore them. They're not known for being nice," she breathes. Pulling me beside her and directing me towards the stairs.

But ignoring them is easier said than done. Walking past them, I throw up a prayer for patience so that I don't knock the pathetic satisfied smiles from their faces.

One Mississippi. Two Mississippi. Three Mississippi. Just breathe, Zoe. Just breathe. They're not worth it.

I repeat my mantra until I'm out the front door.

The walk is quiet and the air is tense. I know Emma wants to comfort me, but she's hesitant because she doesn't know how. All I need is silence right now. All I need is a moment to hold it together before it all falls apart.

His girlfriend died of cancer.

His girlfriend died of cancer.

I had cancer.
It must be some twisted joke.
Project.
Replacement?
Charity case?

27

JESSE

I grab my phone, checking it for the hundredth time. No new messages. Throwing it into my gym bag, I get ready to hit the field for practice.

For some reason, I can't shake the feeling that something's wrong.

I haven't spoken to Zoe much over the last week. For anyone else, that's normal, but for us it's not. We talk every day. It's been like that since the day I met her—every day since we became friends. Even though she said she wanted to spend time with Emma this week, I've still sent her a few messages today to check in, but she hasn't responded.

It feels so wrong to not talk to her. It's almost like a part of me is missing.

"Get your ass outside, Falcon," Coaches' voice booms from behind me.

"Yes, sir." Shutting my locker, I join the others.

Coach blows the whistle—practice is finally over.

If I didn't love this game, if this game didn't help keep me sane, I would've dropped it a long time ago.

This week, I'm glad I have practices to push me past the point of exhaustion. I crave the pain that comes from it because I needed to hurt physically to avoid thinking about all the other ways in which I was hurting.

"Are you okay?" Chase asks as I come out of the locker room shower.

"Yeah," I say, throwing the towel on the bench and putting on some sweatpants.

"You sure?" he presses and I know why.

"Just another year."

He gives me a sympathetic look. "You know we're here if you need us, right?"

"Yup," I respond, watching Chase walk away without saying anything else. I think this is the time of year when he talks to me the most because he wants me to know he cares.

I hear my phone *ping* with a notification, and I quickly search the depths of my bag to find it. When I pull it out, I see Zoe's name displayed across the notification screen.

And just like that, an invisible weight is lifted from my shoulders. Unlocking my phone, I read her text.

Zoe: Can we talk?

That's all the message says, and I wonder if there is something wrong after all.

Me: Of course. Do you want me to come over?

I type out the words quickly and press send. I'm too impatient though, and send a follow up.

Me: I can be there in 15.

Zoe: Sure.

On any other day, a message like this one wouldn't raise red flags, but on a day like today, and after not talking properly to her for almost a week, something tells me I should be worried.

ZOE

Bracing myself for a conversation I wouldn't have dreamed of having, I head down to the lobby. I know Jesse said he'd meet me here in fifteen minutes, but I don't want to have this conversation inside my apartment, or even in my building. What I need is neutral territory.

I sit on the front steps, waiting for him to arrive. When he finally does, he's wearing sweatpants and a sweater with the school logo on it. He must've come straight from practice. As he approaches me, he smiles widely like he's extremely happy to see me.

As if he actually cares about me.

Like I truly mean something to him.

The joke's on me.

Taking a deep breath, I stand up and walk towards him, stopping him from coming any closer.

"Hey," he says, leaning in for a hug.

I sidestep his attempt and cross my arms. "Hey."

He frowns. "Is something wrong?"

"I don't know yet." I want to give him the benefit of the doubt.

"What do you mean?" he says.

I start walking away from my building, praying he follows. I don't know where I'm going, and I don't care. I just know I need to have this conversation and I don't like what the outcome may be.

He follows me cautiously, allowing me the time to gather my thoughts.

"I'm going to ask you a series of questions, and I need you to answer them directly and honestly," I tell him, holding myself together while the world him and I have lived in for the last few months threatens to collapse. Knowing this, I don't allow myself a moment to slow down and let things catch up to me. We walk side-by-side and I make it a point to look straight ahead and avoid his eyes —the eyes that have withheld the truth from me for far too long.

He stops me, guiding me to face him. "Are you okay?"

I give in and look at him. His eyes search my own for a sign of hurt, injury, or pain. I can tell he's trying to assess what's going on, but I give nothing away. I school my expression like the best poker players.

"I will be," I tell him, because I will. I've gotten through worse. "Yes or no answers only, okay?" I add, turning from him and walking towards the quad.

"Zo, you're scaring me."

I can't prolong this conversation any longer. I stop, turning to face him.

"There's nothing to be scared of; I just need answers."

He shifts his weight from one foot to another, and I know he's thinking about a million different scenarios.

I start off easy. "Do you have a girlfriend?"

"No."

"Have you ever had a girlfriend?"

"Yes."

"Any serious relationships?"

He lifts his brows, confused. "One," he says. "Why are you asking me this?"

"Did she die?" I cut straight to it and he flinches. I kick myself for not being sensitive enough. Still, if true, this isn't something I should've found out through sorority girls gossiping behind my back. This is something he should've told me.

"Um..." His eyes latch onto mine, searching for clues. He clears his throat and adds, "Yes" in a whisper so low that I almost miss it. I can see the pain in his eyes and for a brief moment, I feel the desire to bring my arms around him—to comfort him. But I hold onto that small sliver of doubt that keeps wondering if he's been using me. Does he only see me as a charity case? Whatever the answer, I want to hear it straight from his lips.

I inhale deeply, asking the question that could—will—destroy it all. "Did she have cancer?"

"She did," he says matter-of-factly.

I push a little further for clarification. For more. "Did she have ALL?"

"Yes."

They were right. I wanted them to be wrong, but they were right.

"Why didn't you tell me about her?" The weakness in my voice betrays the tough exterior I'm trying to project.

He stares at me, crossing his arms defensively this time. "I didn't think I needed to."

I realize he's not one bit sorry for withholding that information from me.

"You start hanging out with someone who has the same cancer your girlfriend died of and you don't think it's important to mention it?" I feel like I'm shouting, but my words have no strength behind them.

"No, I didn't. I don't see why I need to share that with anyone," he snarls, and I take a step back.

"You don't see why you being with me looks suspicious?"

He wipes his hands on his pants. He's on edge, and I'm nudging him closer.

"Why would me being with you be suspicious?"

"Because your girlfriend had cancer!"

I'm walking on glass and something is bound to break—most likely, me.

"A lot of people have cancer," he says, frustrated. His bag crashes to the cement path and I look around to make sure no one else can hear this conversation. This is something I need to know, but the rest of the world can do without.

"You're missing the point."

He pulls at the hair on the back of his head. "Then spell it out for me, Zoe, because I'm tired of trying to figure it out."

"Isn't it odd that we're..." I lose the courage I had earlier because maybe I shouldn't be mad at him for this. Maybe I've been overthinking what we are. Nothing.

"We're what?"

"It feels like you being with me was all a lie. You talking to me. Me thinking you liked me..." The words tumble out of my mouth in an uncontrollable wave.

"I don't understand why you'd think that," he says, my heart breaking at his admission.

"It feels like you talking to me was your way of trying to replace her," I spit it out. That's my fear—that I'm the replacement for his dead girlfriend.

"No. That's not... I didn't... We aren't..."

We aren't even on the same page here, are we?

"What made you want to be my friend? What made you want to spend so much time with me? What made you want to hold my hand?" I ask all the questions that have been running through my mind at once. He *should have* told me about her.

"I... I just saw you and I can't explain it... I was drawn to you."

Drawn to me? At hospital?

"Did she—" I stop and look away so that the tears threatening to spill over stay at bay. "Was she at the same hospital as me?" I ask. He looks at me like I'm a fragile object that can break at any moment, and then, with a subtle nod of his head, the tears I've been holding back start to fall.

"Do I remind you of her?" I ask, wiping the tears away.

"Zoe..."

"Do I?" I press, my tone harsher.

"A little, yes, but—"

"*God!*" I laugh humorlessly. "Are you even over her?"

"I... I don't know," he says, fisting his hair.

"Why are you with me?"

"I don't... know. I like you. I like spending time with you."

I scoff. "Those girls were right, you know? To you, I'm just a charity case. That's all I've been to you."

"You're not a charity case..."

"You do know that being with me won't bring her back, right?" That's the last thing I hurl at him as I turn around and walk back to my dorm.

He doesn't know what he wants.

And I won't stand here and wait for him to figure it out.

28

JESSE

Being with me won't bring her back.

Those are the words that have been replaying like a bad song on repeat for the last week. Those were the words she chose as she closed herself up to me and walked away.

I slam my head back against the headstone I'm leaning against. How could I've been so stupid, so blind?

I know that being with Zoe won't bring back Hayley.

But I can't help wondering if Zoe was right. Maybe some part of me felt that being with her could make up for losing Hayley?

It's not completely irrational. Fucked up, sure, but not impossible.

I think even a psychologist would agree.

Why else would I fall for someone at the same hospital, on the same floor, suffering the same disease that took away Hayley? If not trying to live my relationship with Hayley through Zoe, then what the hell was I doing?

I don't want to believe that this—me and Zoe—has all been a lie concocted in my mind. I don't want to believe that I'd be such a fucked-up individual to use her that way.

But if that isn't the case, then why didn't I ever put words to my feelings. Why didn't I ask her to be my girlfriend?

I leave the cemetery, driving straight back to the house. Whenever I usually come to see Hayley, I go home and feel at ease, but not today. Today, I'm wired.

I drive a little too fast and get home way too quickly. Parking against the curb, I get out of the car, slamming the door behind me, and walk towards the house. Letting myself in, I'm met with silence, which is not what I expected. There's never silence in this house.

I head over to the kitchen, grab a Gatorade, and then head to the living room. Dropping down onto the couch, I put my feet up and switch on the TV, ready to watch something to drown my thoughts.

My plan is interrupted, though, when my phone rings.

"Dude, where are you?" Zack asks.

"Home, why?" I ask, using as few words as possible.

"Because practice is about to start, and Coach is going to be pissed!" he tells me. No wonder the house was quiet. I must've forgotten about practice with the rollercoaster of a life I've been living this past week.

"Crap, I'll ... I'm on my way." I stand up, hauling ass to my room to get my workout bag.

"How could you forget?" he asks, and the only answer I want to give him is Zoe. Zoe is taking up so much room in my mind that I apparently have none left for anything else.

Instead, I reply, "Don't worry about it."

"Seriously, you've been off these past few days. Actually, now that I think about it, I haven't seen our girl around," Zack says, referring to Zoe. It's no surprise her absence is notable and so is my piss-poor mood.

"She's not our girl," I retort, taking the steps downstairs two at a time.

"You know what I mean, Jesse," he says.

Yeah, I knew what he meant. Zoe already felt like she was part of our family...

So why the hell didn't I do something to make her stay?

I lock the front door behind me and get in my car, shoving my bag onto the seat beside me.

"I'm on my way," I tell him, switching the subject.

"If Coach asks, I'll tell him you had some premed stuff to deal with, but hurry up," he says, and I can hear the voices of my teammates in the background.

"Thanks." He's always had my back. He may not know everything, but that doesn't stop him from being there for me.

"Again," Coach yells as we run laps around the field. With each completed lap, I push myself a little further—try to run a little faster. Every drill Coach calls gives me the opportunity to take out all of my frustrations on my body. I know I'll hurt tomorrow, but I need this today.

Being with me won't bring her back.

Every time I hear those words, I push harder. Run faster. Anything to get them out of my head.

Football practice ends a few hours later. The only thing I'm grateful for is the opportunity to work out and forget what's happening in the real world. While I was working hard on the field, Zoe wasn't on my mind. The moment I stopped though, she consumed my every thought once again.

Zack comes up to where I'm standing in front of the locker assigned to me. "Are you good?"

"Yeah, fine."

"You don't really look fine."

"You don't look so great yourself," I joke, hoping to distract him from asking more.

"That's a lie. I always look great," he says. "But all jokes aside..."

"What?"

"What's going on between you and Zoe?"

"Nothing."

"I thought you guys were starting to... you know?" He waits for me to finish his sentence.

"We were friends." I say it in past tense, flinching when the words leave my mouth.

"You guys are more than friends," he argues.

I wish it were true.

"What makes you say that?" I ask.

"Shit, if we're gonna have a conversation about feelings we're gonna need to go for a drink."

"You're the one that wanted to talk!"

"Because I'm a good asshole. I'm gonna hit the shower real quick," he says, "You should too; you stink."

I follow him into the showers. "Where are we going?"

He grins. "Eclipse."

"Do we have to sit and talk about our feelings." I don't know if I can put mine into words, even knowing that this is probably exactly what I need to do.

"We can either talk, or drink so much we forget our names. Either way, you look like you need a friend."

"That doesn't sound half bad." I need a distraction now that practice is over. Maybe a few drinks are just what will get the job done.

"Do you want it to be just us, or do you want the rest of the guys to join us."

"Should I be preparing for an intervention?" I say half-jokingly.

He nods. "If that's what you need, we can do that."

"I don't think a full intervention is necessary just yet."

"Let's just do the two of us then," Zack says, surprising me. He's the type of guy that doesn't settle down with any girl, the guy that teases Colton about being ‘whipped’, yet here he is being extremely caring about my feelings.

“Thanks,” I tell him genuinely, glad to have him in my life.

“Don’t thank me, you’re paying,” he says with a chuckle.

“If that’s the price I must pay.”

He smirks. “My company is expensive.”

These guys have taught me that brothers aren’t always blood.

29

ZOE

The one thing I didn't miss while at the hospital was attending classes, but it's a welcome distraction. I'm buried in homework, with no time for anything else. That's the approach I've taken with the whole Jesse thing—pretend it didn't happen. I won't cry. I won't stay in the dorm moping around. I'm just going to pretend it's all okay until it really is.

Despite how much having my work pile up on my desk sucks, it's really a privilege for me to have it in the first place. I know I'd never choose the hospital over this.

Second chance, new approach. I'm going to start appreciating things more and complaining about them less. Let's see how long that lasts.

I finish typing the last word on the history essay regarding colonization and save the document. I email it to myself, and then throw my folder in my bag. I have a few minutes to go over to the library and print the essay before I turn it in. The professor says if it's not in his hand a minute before class officially starts then it's an automatic F on the assignment.

Rushing out of the room, I slam the door closed behind me and forego the elevator, choosing to take the stairs. I run down the steps like they're on fire. Zooming out of the front door, I run in the direction of the library. I should've started this paper when the professor assigned it instead of waiting for last minute.

If Emma were here right now, she would've said 'I told you so,' and she would be right.

Emma: one. Zoe: zero.

Approaching the student printing center, which is on the first floor of the library, I log on to the nearest computer finding the document I'd emailed to myself, and hit print. As always, I have to run over to another computer and log on there too so that it finally releases my assignment. I watch each page print slowly as I shift my weight from one foot to the other. Six minutes. I have six minutes to get from this end of campus to the other. Six minutes to have this essay in my professor's hand before it's too late.

Five minutes now because the freaking printer is taking forever. For a second, I think it's going to jam, and I swear my heart skips a beat.

Four minutes and the last piece of paper finally prints. Grabbing my ten-page paper, I run over to the stapler and clip it on the top left as quickly as I can. I run out of there because there's no way I'm going to make it otherwise.

Three minutes and I'm outside, running toward the building my class is in.

Two minutes, and I can see the building. My breathing is heavy and I think about how maybe I should spend more time working out at the gym instead of moping over someone that wasn't mine to begin with.

I look down at my watch as my feet keep moving. One minute. One minute, and I'm making my way up the steps and into the building. My adrenaline is peaking, like I've run a marathon.

Thirty seconds, and I can see the door to my classroom. I don't slow my steps because I know the professor wasn't joking when he said it had to be in his hands a minute before class starts.

Finally, I reach the door and walk inside where the professor waits with a hand extended. My heart is beating too fast, my breath escaping me just as quickly. I give the professor the assignment, turn and blink. My head is spinning, the room nothing but a blur. With a gasp, I'm transported back to freshmen year—back to the last time this happened.

BLACK.

All I can see is black—shadows and darkness shifting uneasily. I suck in a shallow breath when the fragments of moments come together to form a very unclear picture behind my eyelids. In one frame, I'm arriving at class handing my professor my essay. In the other, I'm falling to the ground, my body weak. In the third fragment, I hear panicked noises and sounds of people screaming, asking if I'm okay...but I can't answer them. It feels like I'm not there.

The distinct sound of an ambulance rouses me, but despite how much I try, I can't open my eyes. Then, I feel myself being moved.

Finally, everything goes dark again.

I MANAGE TO PRY MY EYES OPEN BRIEFLY AND REALIZE I'M BEING wheeled into a hospital. The smell, the walls, and the sounds reminding me of every time I've been here before. Deja vu. The familiar fear consumes me.

I'm scared.

I'm scared of being here again. I'm terrified I didn't actually get a second chance, but a prolonged first one. I'm afraid I've lost the battle I thought I'd won.

My eyes open and close as I'm taken to the examination room. In there all I can focus on are the overhead lights. The oxygen mask is doing little to ease my breathing, and although there are mouths moving and conversations happening, I can't make anything out.

Water.

Drowning.

I feel like I'm being submerged in the ocean and despite how much I try, I can't get myself to come back up. I can't get myself to find air, to breathe. So, I give up. I stop trying. That's when I feel myself lose grip of my reality and give in to the darkness once again—the darkness that beckons me.

JESSE

I GRAB MY COFFEE FROM THE STUDENT WORKER AT THE CAFÉ AND START walking toward the table where the guys are chatting. On the way, I pass by Emma, who's sitting with her nose buried in a book.

"Hey," I say, giving her a little wave. I don't know if she'll reciprocate, especially if Zoe told her everything that happened between us.

She glances up, gives me a curt nod and returns to her story. Well, at least she didn't throw the damn book at me.

"Hey! Did you hear about your roommate?" someone says to Emma as I walk by the table. Instantly, my feet are planted in place. I'm hit with a gut feeling, a familiar feeling, that something's wrong. I've felt this unease all morning and I can feel it intensify now. It's the same feeling I had when Zoe didn't message me back. The feeling I couldn't shake when I was headed to the hospital to see Hayley that day.

"What about my roommate?" Emma bites back, ready to defend her friend.

"She passed out in class this morning!"

"She *what?*" I interrupt, the coffee falling from my hands and dropping to the ground.

The girl speaking to Emma looks at me, frowning. "Yeah, Zoe fainted in class."

"What happened?" I'm infuriated by the lack of information I'm getting, and by the look on Emma's face, she is too.

"She was handing the professor her assignment then, all of a sudden, it was lights out. She was gone."

"Where did they take her? Where is she now?" I demand.

"How is she?" Emma asks at the same time I do.

"The ambulance came in. I'm surprised you didn't hear it." I'm seething and this girl is acting like it's a damn joke.

"Which hospital?" I ask, but I've already come up with the answer. If the ambulance picked her up, they would've taken her to the General hospital. They'd have seen her medical history and transferred her over to the Children's Hospital.

This can't be happening. She can't be...

"I don't know. I think they just take you to the nearest hospital."

Before she can finish her sentence, I'm running out of the café. It's only when I get to the parking lot that I realize my car isn't here; I didn't drive today.

"I got you," Colton says from behind me, running straight to his car.

"Thank you," I answer, thinking the absolute worst case scenario right now. She fainted. She passed out.

That's a symptom of relapse, the voice inside my head tells me—the same voice that didn't leave my side when Hayley was losing her fight.

"Get in," Colton says, and I'm a little shocked to see Chase and Emma already in the backseat. Everything is a bit of a blur. I sit back, foot tapping, headache building, and watch as Colton speeds in the direction of the hospital.

Zoe.

Please be okay.

You can't leave me.

"It's going to be okay," Chase says, comforting me. For some reason, I realize it's the nicest tone he's ever used. That's not good. It means he's thinking the worst too, otherwise he'd be telling me to calm the hell down.

"It'll be fine." Colton echoes his best friend's sentiments. I don't say anything. I just sit here uncomfortably and drown in the emotions fighting to overtake me.

Worry.

Fear.

Anger.

I feel all of these emotions at once.

Fuck cancer.

Why have we figured out so much shit, but not a cure for it yet?

She needs to live.

She can't relapse.

This can't happen.

Not again.

I shut my eyes, trying to muster up some sort of inner strength. I tell myself this is different, but it does nothing to relieve the feeling that I'm walking a tight rope and one misstep means I lose everything.

One wrong move and I lose the only person who makes me feel things I thought had died with Hayley.

Fuck.

She can't leave me.

Not like this.

Not thinking the worst of me.

Not thinking I was just using her to get over Hayley.

That couldn't be further from the truth. I wasn't using her to get over Hayley. I didn't want to get over Hayley, I just did.

Zoe was healing me.

Zoe was giving me life.

She needs to know I want her.

I need her.

I love her.

I'm *in love* with her.

The realization hits me at the same time that Colton's foot hits the break in front of the hospital. I fly out of the front passenger seat, heading straight through the double doors and into the emergency room. Running over to the receptionist, I blurt out Zoe's name, demanding to know where she is. She must've recognized me because she tells me where to find her.

I run up the stairs because the elevator would be too slow. My vision is blurry, my heart hammering against my ribs.

Not again.

I make it to the oncology floor, where Zoe has spent the last year either living or visiting. I don't walk, I run. I run to where I know she's supposed to be waiting. There are no words I have prepared. No fancy speech. Nothing. The only thing I care about is her. I throw a prayer up to the same God I have prayed to many times before asking for healing. For health. For safety. Though I'm skeptical, he'll listen.

Five doors, three doors, two doors, one. I come face-to-face with the room Zoe is in. I take a deep breath, forcing the negative thoughts out of my head and open the door.

Opening this door is like reliving a nightmare I've barely survived before. Like last time, the room is spotless. The bed is made. There are no creases, and no flowers, pictures, or active machines. Nothing.

Dead.

Dead like when you showed up after class, eager to talk to Hayley and tell her everything that happened at school so you could see her smile as she lived vicariously through you.

Dead as her lifeless body in the casket.

Dead.

No. I won't accept it. I refuse to accept the same fate twice. But even as I battle the voices inside of my head, my knees give out and I fall to the floor.

"Zoe..." Her name falls from my lips like another prayer—praying for a different reality—but I know that it's pointless.

30

ZOE

"Someone's here to see you," my mother says as she lets herself into my bedroom. She's sequestering me here against my will for the rest of the week. Who would've thought that exerting myself running would result in me passing out? Not me.

"Who?" I ask as my mother stands there looking giddy. I wonder who it could be. Emma, maybe? She must've heard what happened by now; I'm sure the news made it around the whole school by the time I was placed in the back of the ambulance.

"You'll see," she says cryptically.

"Mom!" I call to her retreating figure, but she ignores me. I hear voices out in the hallway and I lean forward a little, trying to catch any clues as to who it might be.

I'm stunned when I see a familiar face at the door. Jesse knocks on the door frame awkwardly. "Mind if I come in?"

For a moment, I'm happy until I remember the last time we spoke. I feel my smile drop.

When I say nothing, he lingers near the door, reminding me of the first time I met him.

"Hey," he says quietly.

I keep my eyes lowered, not ready to get lost in his unwavering, questioning gaze. "Hello."

"How are you doing? Are you okay?"

"I'm fine." My words are clipped—to the point.

"Are you sure? What happened?"

I glance up, feeling disrespectful for not looking at him while he speaks. "Nothing."

"It's obviously not 'nothing.' You fainted in class. An ambulance took you to the hospital, and now you're in bed. Something happened," he says, frustrated, and I search his face.

"I was trying to turn something in on time, but I was late so I ran. I guess I wasn't supposed to do that and that's why I fainted. Dr. Roman said I'm fine."

He sighs out loud and neither one of us says anything else. I shift uncomfortably on the bed, hating how thick the tension is as the silence stretches between us.

"What do you want, anyway?" I spit out. It's nice that he showed up to make sure I was okay, but that's not what I need from him. His internship is over, and so is our friendship.

"I wanted to make sure you were okay," he says, walking slowly toward me and taking a seat on the corner of my bed. I lean back against the headboard, watching him—keenly aware of the way his chest rises and falls with each breath, the way the color returns to his cheeks.

"I'm okay." At least physically. Emotionally, it's a whole different story.

"What happened? I didn't get many details at the hospital."

My eyes widen. "You *went* to the hospital?"

"Yeah, I ..." he starts, stops then scratches his head as if debating how much to say.

"I'm okay," I tell him, feeling the need to reassure him.

"You ended up in the hospital..." he says waiting for me to explain.

"They did some tests, but everything is okay."

"No relapse?" he asks and I realize his mind went to the same place mine did—worst case scenario.

"Nope," I answer. I was just as relieved as he looks now. I wasn't sure I'd win if I had to fight cancer again.

"God, you have no idea how worried I was at the thought of you being in a hospital again," he says, and it's followed by an intake of breath that looks almost painful.

"I have an idea."

"You still don't know what it feels like—to have someone you love lie in a hospital bed, fighting cancer." He gets up and starts to pace. "You don't know what it feels like to find out that the person you love...that the girl you love ended up in the hospital," he finally spits out and I stare at him blankly.

"You don't know what it's like to drive to the hospital and run all the way up to where she's supposed to be," he continues, "and find that she's not there anymore. You have no idea what I felt!" His voice has risen, cracking slightly at the end. He stops pacing, turns toward me, and meets my gaze. Through his eyes, he shows me the pain, struggle, fear, and worry. I see everything I've felt in the past couple of hours.

"Yes, I lost my high school girlfriend to cancer. I should've told you about her, but I didn't want to. I was trying to hold on to the past. For so long, she was the center of my world. For so long, she was the person I was doing everything for, my motivation," he says and I fight the tears threatening to fall.

Why is he here? Why is he telling me all this now? Why is he breaking me again?

"She was the only person I ever wanted to be with. And when she passed away, I didn't think I'd ever be with anyone else. That's what I told myself. But, when I went inside that hospital room and you weren't there..."

He stops pacing and sits beside me, close enough to touch me if he wanted.

"I realized it was a lie," he whispers, his eyes lifting to meet mine. "I've been through this before, and I didn't think I could ever come close to feeling what I felt the day I found out Hayley had succumbed to her cancer. But I guess I was wrong."

Reaching out, he touches my cheek, a deep breath leaving him like a sigh. Instinctively, I draw closer to him, desperate for his touch.

"I felt it all over again today. I hadn't realized I'd moved on, made peace with Hayley for leaving me, until a few days ago. I'm an idiot for not seeing it sooner—for dragging my feet. But today when I thought you...when I thought your life was in danger, I had an epiphany..."

"What was it?" I finally ask, eager to hear what he's got to say, but also scared at what his next words could be.

He doesn't look away. "That I'm in love with you."

"You thought I was going to die and *then* you realized you loved me?" I pull away abruptly, his hand falling onto his lap. "How do you know you weren't just thinking of Hayley?" I add. Her name sounds foreign on my lips. Asking him this hurts me more than I thought it would, but I have to know. I love him, and it didn't take long for me to realize that, but I cannot live in the shadow of his girlfriend. I can't settle for less than what I deserve.

I refuse to.

"I know because there was not one damn moment when I wasn't thinking about you. Goddammit, the last few weeks have been hell. Stopping myself from messaging you, calling you, finding you was fucking torture. And then hearing about you being at the hospital from someone else made me realize I never want to not be there for you."

"Like you were for Hayley," I say in a low whisper. It still feels like he's trying to replace her.

"You don't get it." He gets up from the bed. "I was there for Hayley, yes, but I want to be here for you. Now. And before you say anything," he says, stopping my protests, "when I heard about you this morning, it wasn't Hayley I was thinking about as I ran to the parking lot. Or when the guys drove me to the hospital. Or when I ran up the stairs and straight into the room they told me you'd be in.

It was *you*. Walking into that room and finding it empty shattered me. I thought you'd lost your battle like Hayley had, and I felt that loss so profoundly that I didn't think I could go through it all again." He takes a seat again, framing my face in his hands.

"I want you to understand that I loved her, that some part of me still does, and probably always will."

I close my eyes at his words, not wanting him to see how much they hurt.

"But I *need* you. I'm *in love* with you. I can't see myself with anyone but you."

As he says this, I open my eyes and the tears I've been holding back begin to fall. He brushes them away gently with his fingers.

"I may be a little rusty at the whole boyfriend thing. I haven't dated anyone since her; I've never wanted to," he says with a nervous chuckle. I just listen to that sound, feeling the softness of his hands on my skin. "But I want to try. You make me want to try. You make me want to fight."

"You really want to give this a try?" I ask, my voice vulnerable as I give him the choice I don't really want him to make.

"I want this more than you think." The words leave his mouth with absolute certainty. "Do you want to be with me?" he asks, moving so close to me, I feel like he's going to finally kiss me.

I answer with the same assurance he had. "I've wanted to be with you for a long time now."

"I've wanted to be with you too; it just took me a little longer to admit it to myself," he says with a smile.

"Think we should give it a try?" I ask him once again. The logical part of me doesn't want to believe this—that he wants to be with me, and I know it's because I don't want to get hurt again. Logic battles with my emotions, but it's my heart that's desperate to take control.

"If we don't give it a try, I'm going to spend the rest of my life as a miserable asshole," he says and I laugh. His hands begin caressing my cheeks once again, bringing the comfort only he provides.

"We wouldn't want to make you a miserable asshole now, would we? Doctors are supposed to be nice," I joke, the weight lifting as my heart soars.

"Does that mean you'll give this—us—a chance?"

"Only if you really want to."

He doesn't answer me with words. Instead his lips are on mine, connecting us in a way I've been craving for a while.

"God, why did we wait so long to do this?" he asks, putting words to my thoughts. His hands find my hair, and his tongue moves along with mine for the first time. It's like a slow dance. And even though it's all new, it feels like we've been doing it forever.

"Because you didn't take initiative," I respond between kisses.

"I'll make sure I do that more often. We have a lot of catching up to do," he answers and I laugh. Then, his lips are back on mine and the rest of the world fades away.

Someone clears their throat in the doorway. "You've had your turn. Can I see my roommate now?" I hear Emma say.

"Shit, I forgot you were in the car too!" Jesse says turning toward the door where Emma stands.

"I figured you did," she says walking the rest of the way into the room.

"I'm sorry, I was—" Jesse starts, but is interrupted.

"I saw what you were doing," she teases. "Just in case you also forgot, Colton and Chase were in the car too. And now they're both awkwardly sitting in the living room being grilled by Zoe's dad," she says, then looks at me and smiles.

31

JESSE

Every heavy step I take brings me closer to Hayley's grave, but I keep moving.

It's time.

Finding my usual spot and getting comfortable next to her headstone, I once again engage in my ritual of replacing her flowers. Lilies. Bright and beautiful just like her.

The ones here are a little more recent, which tells me someone else has come to visit her.

I'm not the only one.

She's not alone. She was loved by many—still is.

I take a giant deep breath in and release it slowly, preparing myself for this conversation.

It's time.

"Hi, Hayley," I say cautiously to the girl who has controlled my every thought for years. "I know you can't hear me, but as always, I'll make a fool of myself by talking anyway."

I pause for a moment. "I actually came here today because I'm following your advice—the advice I know you'd give me if you could actually talk." I look up at the sky, which is surprisingly light and blue. There are no clouds in sight, and the sun is shining bright. It feels like Hayley is smiling down at me.

The weight I've been feeling seems to disappear then, and a peace takes over my body. This is right. This is what she wants me to do.

"Remember that girl, the one I kept talking to you about as a sort of side comment in our conversations? The one I vented to you about last time I was here? Well, I'm kind of, sort of..." I pause, trying to figure out how to say this.

"I'm... I think I'm in love with her. No, I don't think—I know. She said I was trying to replace you with her. I'll admit at first I was pissed. Then I started to believe her words too. I loved you so much that I couldn't imagine anyone else taking your spot. I didn't want to give anyone else your place. And I haven't. I won't."

"You have your forever place in my heart, but Zoe... Zoe's got her own now, too. I fell in love with her because of who she is. She makes me feel things I haven't felt in a while. I mean, the moment I thought something was wrong with her, I rushed to get to her. I wondered whether she would live, whether cancer would take her life—take her away from me. I think that's when I realized I was starting to move on. Without knowing it, I'd opened my heart up to someone else."

"I hope you're okay with that." I look up once again seeking confirmation. I spot a few birds take flight at the same time and I laugh out loud.

Very cliché, Hayley.

"Anyway, I've been thinking about this for a while. And once I finally got Zoe to understand I fell in love with her for her, I knew I had to have this talk with you." My hands go to my jeans and I clean off the sweat I feel building.

"I knew you weren't going to hate me for moving on. I knew you'd want me to. I just didn't think I could do it. But with Zoe, I can. I know it's a weird thing to say, but I think the two of you would've been great friends. I wish she could've met you when you still smiled." I look away from Hayley's grave and back at the girl who's been standing on the gravel path waiting for me.

Her red hair is just below her chin now and moves with the wind. Her eyes fix on mine, and she gives me a reassuring smile. She gives me the strength I need.

"Better late than never, right?"

I motion for Zoe to join me and she does. She takes measured steps, walking the path I've walked many times before—the path I'll continue to walk every once in a while, because even though I'm moving on, moving on doesn't mean forgetting people in the past. It means still caring about them, but also allowing yourself to care about others, too.

And I care about Zoe so much.

I didn't even see how this smart-mouthed sassy girl, who was fighting for her life, was fighting my battle too.

ZOE

I CAREFULLY WALK TO WHERE MY DARK-HAIRED, MUSCULAR, STRONG, gorgeous man sits on the ground looking as small as ever.

I know this is probably not easy for him, but it's something he wanted to do—something he needed to do.

Even from here, I can tell that getting this chance is doing him good. On the drive over, he looked tense. His jaw was locked, his eyes lost somewhere in the past—distant. He was worried, and I knew this was going to be difficult for him. He was finally letting go of a very important part of his life—a motivating part—and while I was jealous at first, I've since come to my senses. Jesse loved her. He loved her well, and the same disease that almost took me, took her.

Instead of cowering and giving in to helplessness, he's dedicating his life to try and help. To try and find a cure. Because while cancer took Hayley away, it didn't take me. And if it's up to Jesse, in the future, it won't take anyone else.

His eyes find mine once again as I near the grave, and what I see in them makes me release the breath I've been holding ever since we got here. He looks happy. Relieved. Content—ready to take on whatever else the world has got to throw at him.

He extends his hand to me and I thread my fingers with his. An easy-going smile is on his lips, and I think it's the happiest I've seen him.

"This should've happened a lot earlier," he says, getting up.

"I think this is as a good a time as any," I respond, placing my hand on his shoulder and signaling him to sit back down as I join him on the ground.

He looks at me like I'm the most amazing and precious thing he's ever seen. Well, the joke's on him because he's been the best part of my year. He saw me at my worst and remained. He saw me cry, scream, yell, and suffer, but he stayed with me when he could've just as easily walked away. He was fighting his own battles, which I didn't see. And when I got a glimpse, instead of fighting for him—fighting for us—I ran.

"Hayley, this is the girl I've been telling you about," he states by way of introduction.

"Hi, Hayley, I'm Zoe. I've heard a lot about you."

"You know she can't hear you, right?" Jesse says with a smirk.

"She may," I respond, looking up at the sky. I hope she's heard his every word, his every story, his every plea.

And I can tell by the look in his eyes that he hopes for the same.

EPILOGUE

ZOE

"My, my, my, what progress we've made since the last time we hung out here," Kaitlyn mocks from her seat in front of the fire. We're back at the House, celebrating the fact that the guys are going to the National Championship...again.

This celebration is a little different though. "Definitely. There's not a rager happening just through those doors," I say pointing at the door to the kitchen. Inside the house, the rooms are empty. It's quiet. The school opened up the ballroom and threw a party there to celebrate the team making it for the second time. A few of us skipped it.

Kaitlyn gives me a long look. "That's not what I mean, and you know it. I mean you cuddled up with future doctor over there," she says, pointing at us. We're sharing a chair, a blanket thrown over us to protect us from the cold night air.

"You missed out on prime real estate here," Jesse jokes, pointing at himself.

"No, thanks," Kaitlyn shakes her head.

"Pay up, Kaitlyn!" Mia jumps in.

"I know, I know," Kaitlyn says, resigned.

"What do you owe her for?" Colton asks, eager to figure out what's happening.

That makes two of us.

"I told her that by the end of the year, these two would be a thing!" Mia exclaims.

"You bet on us getting together?" I ask.

"Of course I did. I've never seen Jesse look happier than when he's with you," Mia says, and I swear I almost melt at her words.

"So, wait, you bet against us becoming a thing?" Jesse asks Kaitlyn.

"No, I thought you guys would get together a lot earlier. Thanks for being super freaking slow. You owe me a hundred bucks," Kaitlyn deadpans. I wish this would've happened sooner too, but I think it happened when it needed to.

"So, how are we spending our hundred dollars, babe?" Colton asks Mia.

"*We* sounds like a lot of people," she retorts. "I'm going for frozen yogurt with my girls."

Everyone erupts into laughter.

"Wow, them over me, huh?" Colton asks, his hand going to his chest like he just took a bullet to the heart.

"When did you become so soft?" Mia teases, abandoning her seat and joining him in his.

"Only with you, babe. Only with you," he replies and I can tell he means it.

"Where's Chase?" I ask, curious to know why the sixth person at our bon fire is missing. Although we haven't done this in a couple of weeks, we've done it enough times that it's become an unspoken tradition—beer, bon fire, and a star-lit sky with Mia, Colton, Kaitlyn, Chase, Jesse, me and sometimes, like today, Emma.

"He's keeping an eye on things at the party," Colton says as he covers Mia with a blanket.

"I bet he is." Kaitlyn's tone is bitter, but I think I'm the only one that hears her.

"You doing okay, Red?" Jesse whispers in my ear, pulling me closer.

"I'm perfect," I say. I've been healthy and I'm not afraid of getting sick again. It's still possible, but I don't think about it anymore. I have faith that I'm going to be okay, especially with this man by my side.

Colton and Mia stand up, their fingers intertwined. "We're going to head out," Mia says to the group.

"Seriously? The night is young!" Kaitlyn whines.

"I'm taking my girl out," Colton says, kissing the back of her hand.

"You can come with if you want!" the ever-sweet Mia offers.

"I'm good," Kaitlyn replies. "Hey Emma?"

"Yeah?" Emma says, looking up from her e-reader. Yes, she brought it with her tonight.

"Let's go celebrate the end of the year!" Kaitlyn exclaims, and I look at my roommate, waiting for her to turn down the invitation.

"I thought you weren't partying anymore?" Emma asks, pushing her glasses a little higher up on her nose.

"I've made it a long time without partying. It's the end of the year; let's go have fun!" I watch the exchange take place, wondering if Kaitlyn has the power of persuasion I've lacked.

Emma points at me and Jesse. "Why don't you go with them?"

"Pass," I reply at the same time as Jesse says "No, thanks."

Kaitlyn rolls her eyes. "See, they're lame too."

"On that note, we'll see you guys tomorrow," Mia says, handing Colton the blanket. Together they walk back into the house, Colton's arm winding around her waist.

"I don't know," Emma replies and I'm surprised she's even considering it.

"One night of fun never hurt anyone," Kaitlyn insists. Emma looks at me and Jesse, and then back at Kaitlyn.

"Why not? I'll consider it a social experiment," my roommate says, shocking me.

Kaitlyn practically jumps out of her lawn chair. "Great! Let's go!"

"Where are we going exactly?" Emma asks, and I can tell she's feeling ready to back out.

"We'll just join the rest of the guys," Kaitlyn answers.

"What am I getting myself into?" Emma asks rhetorically as Kaitlyn grabs her by the hand and pulls her to her feet.

"You'll see! Now, let's head over to my place and get ready."

"I'll see you later," Emma says, turning to wave at us as she's lead inside the house by a very determined Kaitlyn.

JESSE

Everyone leaves at once and I'm left with the prettiest girl tucked between my arms. I'm a lucky man, and I don't know what I've done to deserve it—to deserve her.

"I thought they'd never leave," I tell her, holding her closer—feeling the heat of her body next to mine, loving the way her breathing matches my own. She repositions herself on the chair so that she's facing me, and looks at me with love in her eyes.

"Oh yeah?" she asks, her sass on full display. "What for?"

Damn, I love this girl. "So I can have you all to myself," I reply with a grin.

She runs her fingers through my hair. "And now that you have me all to yourself, what are you going to do?"

I lean in closer. "Would you rather I tell you, or show you?" I whisper in her ear.

"You already know the answer." I take her answer as a green light and bring my hands to her beautiful red hair. I bring my lips to hers, kissing her so slowly that I can feel it consuming me.

"I love you," I tell her in between kisses. I'll tell her any chance I can get.

"And I love you," she echoes.

Out here with the stars as our witnesses, I show her how much she means to me because I know actions always speak louder than words.

Even before I could find the words to tell her how I felt—even before I figured it out myself—we both already knew.

Click here to read Zack Hayes' Story!

ABOUT THE AUTHOR

Gianna Gabriela is a small town girl living in the Big Apple. Gianna's always been a writer. Growing up, she would write poems, speeches, and even songs. Still, one day she woke up with a pressing need to write a book. She heeded the desire and now writes stories featuring the brooding heroes you want and the strong heroines you need.

Keep up to date - sign up for Gianna's newsletter

Need more?
Here's what to read next...

Bragan University Series

Better With You (Book #1)
Fighting For You (Book #2)
Falling For You (Book #3)
Better With You, Always (Book #4)

COMING SOON
Waiting For You (Book #5)
Finally With You (Book #6)

The Not Alone Novellas

Not the End (Book #1)
Not the Same (Book #2)

COMING SOON
Not Alone (Book #3)

Stand-Alone

Just Because of You

Made in the USA
Monee, IL
25 August 2020

39333707R00118